AF577415

another story

a novella

By Brian Swann

BOOKS BY BRIAN SWANN

FICTION

The Runner
Elizabeth
Unreal Estate

POETRY

The Whale's Scars
Roots
Living Time
The Four Seasons
The Middle Of The Journey

CHILDREN'S BOOKS

The Fox And The Buffalo
Water Became Bone

TRANSLATIONS

The Collected Poems Of Lucio Piccolo (with Ruth Feldman)
Selected Poetry Of Andrea Zanzotto (with Ruth Feldman)
Shema: Collected Poems Of Primo Levi (with Ruth Feldman)
The Day Is Always New: Selected Poems Of Rocco Scotellaro (with Ruth Feldman)
The Dry Air Of the Fire: Selected Poems Of Bartolo Cattafi (with Ruth Feldman)
Selected Poems Of Tudor Arghezi (with Michael Impey)
Primele Poeme / First Poems Of Tristan Tzara (with Michael Impey)
Euripedes' Phoenissae (with Peter Burian)
The Moon Of the Bourbons: Selected Poems Of Vittorio Bodini (with Ruth Feldman)
On The Nomad Sea: Selected Poems Of Milih Cevdet Anday (with Talat Halman)
Song Of The Sky: Versions Of Native American Poetry
Rome: Danger To Pedestrians, By Rafael Alberti (with Linda Scheer)

EDITING

Currents And Trends: Italian Poetry Today (with Ruth Feldman)
Smoothing The Ground: Essays On Native American Oral Literature

another story

a novella

By Brian Swann

Adler Publishing Company
Rochester, New York

ANOTHER STORY

BY BRIAN SWANN

FIRST EDITION

For information address:

Adler Publishing Company
P.O. Box 9342
Rochester, N.Y. 14604

Cover Design by Leontine Klem

Graphics by Sasha Trouslot / Foxglove Graphics, Inc.

ISBN 0-913623-03-2

Library of Congress Catalog Card No. 83-82475

Printed in the United States of America

Some of this book has appeared, frequently in different shape, in the following journals: *The Agni Review*, *Aspen Anthology*, *Aura Literary/Arts Review*, *Beyond Baroque*, *Carleton Miscellany*, *Center*, *Edgeworks*, *Interstate*, *Invisible City*, *New Boston Review*, *New Orleans Review*, *Newsart/The Smith*, *New York Arts Journal*, *Panache*, *Paris Review*, *Poetry Now*, *Skywriting*, *Story Quarterly*, *Texas Quarterly*, *Wormwood Review*.

With thanks to the NEA for a Fellowship

FIRST

My life is without adventure. I am a creature of habit. Habit has a concentrating effect (as Dr. Johnson said of death). There is too much of everything everywhere. One has to focus on habitual things. There are enough forces for dispersal and distraction.

~

The first thing I hear every morning is falling water.

There is a fountain under my window. A fountain that does not tell the truth. This is the case with most fountains. They are, however, gentle liars.

What it tells are stories that have long been disproven or, worse, dead.

Rivers have long since ceased to tell stories of any kind. Even their laments have become complaints.

The seas still make efforts, aided by what the winds bring. But the winds have been tracked to their lair and, like the Atlantic salmon traced to their spawning grounds on cold Icelandic shelves, will never be the same. The encyclopedias become richer as seas and winds are forced to fabricate their existence. Or empty themselves into ears that have heard wolf once too often. The song the Sirens sung has been recorded. It is nothing special.

As I look down through parted leaves I can see the water in the fountain, leaping up, curling the feathers in its tail like a tall white bird, falling back to origins to gather and rise again.

The fountain under my window that doesn't tell the truth wakes me each morning and lulls me to sleep at night. I see it first and last thing when I part or draw the shades. It is with me all day and a good part of the night. A small fountain, a clever lying little fountain. O fons Bandusiae . . .

~

A watch. I remembered it as I lay in bed one morning after snow had silenced the fountain. The old watch that used to hang from the black silver satin pocket of my grandfather Jim, swinging when he walked. Or stuck plumb deep in his black silver waistcoat pocket, sliding with dignity, infinitesimally, imperceptibly, from side to side in the dark as he rolled slightly in his old walk.

But the back was buckled.

In my mind I pushed the buckled edge down, trying to even it up, make it flush-level. But the other edge kept popping up. I continued this for some time, finally trying to put equal pressure on both edges. When it suddenly occurred to me that I hadn't heard it ticking. To make sure it was working, and worth all the trouble—maybe it was old and dead, the buckling a sign it had succumbed to its own native pressures of time, or foreign forces thought tamed that had twisted it away from perfection—I put a thumbnail under the tipped edge and pried it open like an oyster. Inside all was calm. The wheels were whirring silently, with jerky elasticity. It was an image of quiet efficiency yet with none of the hectic bounce of youth; it was moving with all the grace of the perfect result of the most economical movement.

And the back remained open, buckled.

~

When I get up in the morning I am relentless in my predictability. I always begin the day with a stumble. Stumbling brings the whole being into some sort of balance.

In the night there are statues to keep erect, faces to keep clear, and feet to calm.

Everything is bolted to the floor, for when the things move the floor moves.

The effort is enormous.

By this simple act of stumbling every morning I remind myself of freer possibilities. Picking myself up, I am able to sort out my priorities anew.

Gradually, my life has become a constant stumble. But I do as best I can. At night I am stiff guardian of the tightrope. By day, my effort is to make my stumble look like a walk. This way my grip becomes looser and more secure. As I struggle onward I come to night and shake it through the cool net. What slips through is what I value, though seldom find.

On hands and knees, by day I grope between the highlights on a fallen face and the deepest shadows. I expect everything to fall naturally into place. Often that 'everything' stays a void pushing everything apart.

So I am continually learning my balance among faces. My walking is constant but uncertain. When I slept I used to think I was safe. But now even that perfection I touched is tainted. The faces have taken over the statues, blurring them.

I am learning to deceive. My stumbling has become so expert it looks contrived.

Somewhere there must be a real stumble, a real walk, somewhere a genuine elegance, a full face.

I cannot find them in either of my two houses.

~

As a result, my days frequently seem heavy. Physically heavy. As if a tent is about to collapse. But it never does. There is always one more tent beyond the one about to collapse. That always produces a feeling of great calm.

I am not the only one to feel this way. People hereabouts have trained themselves not to look up, though of course they do, from time to time. That too produces a feeling of great calm. They have been taught since childhood about the tents beyond the tent they could see. There was nothing more to be said on the subject, though there are those who, when they look up, think. They think doubts.

When I was a child, whenever it thundered my grandfather Jim would tell me it was the Devil clomping about in his hobnail boots. Of course I believed him. It still makes more sense, this eerie picture that cannot be pictured, this mind-filling scene too big for the mind. More sense than the rushing about of invisible air and the discharging of electrical currents. What are these? Hypotheses we do not experience but take on trust. Nothing enters the mind. Not like the Devil, thumping about in his boots in another country above us. And beyond that?

Sometimes I have been tempted to believe those who had heard rumors that they didn't exist. Why I didn't, in the end, was because I had heard another story.

Heard one, or dreamed one. In any case, I often think of the illiterate Caedmon, the first English poet, being told by the angel, "Sing me Creation." And I dream of ladders, constantly; angels going up and down them, singing. I always seem to be just coming out of a sleep in which I have dreamed of ladders. At the top of these ladders is all Creation.

~

One day I got up and walked to my window. A head sat under the eaves, a woman's head. She seemed in no discomfort. I opened the window a crack and her voice came clear across the alley. The head bobbed in the wind, a little like a balloon, against the drainpipe.

The house opposite had no windows on the side facing me. I imagined that mine must be the only window facing across to the blank wall. I thought that I did not know the face, though it was not unfamiliar. After she spoke, I immediately forgot what she had said, and had a hard time reconstructing any of the words afterwards. Perhaps she talked of her children. Yes, that was it. Children. But what were they, children? And what were her children to me? I wandered away from the window. A slight draft slipped under it. I knew the head was still there, looking right in at my window which had neither blinds nor curtains. There was no need to hide anything from a blank wall.

I picked up the small fire-extinguisher fixed to the wall beside the kitchen. I shook it. Its rattle convinced me all was well. I moved a book from one end of the shelf to the other. I picked a dead leaf off a philodendron that occupied one corner of the room. I looked back at the window. The lips were still moving, words dribbling off into the wind. I lip-read, but the results meant nothing. The head bounced a little. I realized that without the eaves and drainpipe it would have floated off. A sense of urgency stirred me. On my way back to the window, staring at her eyes, I struck my head against part of the cast-iron staircase that ran up to the bedroom, bare except for a heavy bed; a staircase that twisted like a double helix.

The head was silent when I got to the window again. I pushed the window up and open with great difficulty for it had never been fully opened before. Cold air made me catch my breath. The head, with silent lips, seemed far away. The sadness of the face struck me, as if it had always been looking in windows. I found myself leaning out, trying to reach across and bring the head indoors. But I was yards short. I realized it would only be a matter of minutes before the head was caught in a current and lifted across the impediment, perhaps lodging in a tree, or landing on the sea, or on some empty city roof, or a field.

I leaned out so far I nearly fell. The head started to speak again, but its hair was blowing across its face, and finally blew into its mouth, stopping all words. The wind blew from another direction and the hair whipped back from the mouth. The head and I stood gazing at one another as if we would never stop. I recognized the face, but did not know it. We stared at each other, I from the cover of a room, she out in the open, trapped still.

I remembered the ladder.

SECOND

I lived most of my childhood with my grandparents in England. They seldom spoke to me, though I liked them a great deal. Theirs was a strange house, though. People would come and go unannounced. I never knew who they were and never asked in case I wasn't supposed to know. I was an only child and was often alone in the big house. My grandparents refused to send me to school in case I picked up something from the other kids.

One morning when my grandparents were out, I never knew where, I wandered into my grandmother's parlor. The dark harmonium stood in one corner, and beside the harmonium a door leading to the conservatory. Its leaves pressed against the glass. I could smell the dark dried blood placed round the roots of tomato plants. There was not much light anywhere in the oakpanelled room as I walked over the carpet with its elaborate oriental designs.

There was a woman crouching in front of the conservatory door. I walked closer, slowly. When I could almost have touched her, I reached down instead to pick up a corner of the carpet. There was a pond underneath, with fish. I'd never seen any of this before. The woman looked at me.

"Don't worry," she said. "Look, I can hold one in my hand."

She dipped her hand into the water, and a small flattish fish lay still in her palm.

"You have to know how to handle them," she said. "Piranhas."

THIRD

On those occasions when my grandparents went off for days, sometimes weeks at a time, an insect used to be my constant companion and helper. It helped me get into the house when I forgot my key. It shared my food and even went to bed with me. It was a very special relationship. But one day the insect got lost. I was very miserable. The house seemed so empty. Then a few days later I saw an insect, and thought it was him. But I really knew it wasn't. This insect was larger, and could fly.

FOURTH

One day I was spending time watching some tomatoes, dark red, all sizes. They were falling from the arbor at the bottom of the garden. I was worried that, as they were falling on hard earth, they'd be crushed. But they weren't. I picked some up, and they didn't stain my hands. I took them inside, up to my bedroom. I arranged them on the windowsill.

Then I found I could fly.

I held my breath, stepped out of the window, and floated above the ground.

My grandparents could not hear me when I called to them.

I decided to get them to fly too. In the night.

FIFTH

On those occasions when my father visited, he'd sometimes take me (and my mother too, if she was there) off on trips. Like the one to the ranch-like wooden house he won on a TV game show.

When I got tired or irritated I'd leave the house and go to sleep in his hammock in the woods.

I used to ask strange questions in those days. I remember asking my mother: "What do you do when you get constipated? For relief."

She laid down her knitting.

"*He* sticks his finger up his hole," she said, leaving.

My father came back in.

"There's no need to put your hammock out in the open, you know," he said. "Just put a couple of screws in the beams up there and sling it between them. Like we do in the Merchant Navy."

"But the beams come out of the house on the other side," I replied. "The hammock could just as well be slung from there."

"Come outside, then," said my father, "and you'll see why not. Come outside anyhow. I have a present for you. Something I picked out for you special."

We went outside. There was a small herd of ponies, sleek and brown.

"One of them is yours," said my father. "That one."

But I didn't like "that one". A fat cowboy pony. I held out my hand to one with a long white face. An Indian pony, an Appaloosa. It came towards me, pursing its velvet lips. It began to suck my hand like a calf. I was afraid and stepped back. My father knew I'd choose this horse. I had always been afraid of Palominos. They don't look natural.

SIXTH

I was ten, precisely.

One day I was walking round the ornamental lake in the park. Then I decided to clamber over the monuments and statues, especially over their faces.

I reached a large clock with two second hands: second hand one, and second hand two. The latter was large and fast, and blocked my access to any further climbing and clambering.

Up till then, all my climbing had been done to waltz time. One two three, one two three. Now it changed to a polka, as the loudspeaker announced the guest appearance of Marie-Louise Bloch, the famous dancer.

But almost immediately the loudspeaker corrected itself. "The next event is a swim," it boomed. "In freestyle time."

I was ten, precisely. On the dot. And I could not swim.

SEVENTH

I don't suppose I was what you'd call a lively or adventurous child. But I was imaginative, and a born liar. I was also nosey. I always suspected there were secrets all around me, if I just knew where to look. (As I grew older I became surer there were secrets, all the more intriguing since I had never found out any more than the one I am about to tell you).

It was a usual kind of Spring day: jittery and nervous. I waited till my father was at work and my mother out shopping. Then I went up to their bedroom and began my usual search for secrets, a search which up till then had yielded some Durex and a sex manual which had big words and no pictures. I started safely, opening the top left drawer of the dressing-table. Rolls of small candies, assorted cookies. Nothing secret here. My parents were guilty of simple deceit. I ate selectively and with a view to arrangement. Then I went to where I knew my father kept a bottle of scotch at the back of a drawer, and took a swig that nearly choked me. I was careful to note how much I'd drunk, and went to the bathroom with the bottle to top it up. Putting the bottle back, my hand felt something that hadn't been there the last time. I took out a large book carefully covered with brown paper. I opened the front cover, and an envelope fell out. Inside the envelope were photos.

My mother leaned back on my father's lap, his penis inside her. Another man, young as my parents, in his mid twenties, sat and watched, his long member hanging between his knees. Photos, and more photos. My armpits started to sweat and my hands shook in excitement. My father's penis just coming out of my mother, her hands around it. I checked. I was sure it was about the same size as my own adolescent cock, handsome from the back where the urethra was long, and curved down to the balls. There were photos of the young man inside my mother, and it was all very sociable and calm. I'd always suspected it. The faded photos continued in another envelope that I found at the back of the book.

My father was in the Merchant Navy. Young men, all naked, were bathing on a foreign shore; sunbathing, swimming, hosing down. It all looked as if it had been taken yesterday. And there, yes, there was Trixie and my mother and father, her highcheeked face full of my father's cock. From the shore of a small lake, my mother sat watching. Her eyes seemed to twinkle.

I was recalling all this early today, a Spring day like any other Spring day: jittery and nervous. I hadn't seen my parents for years. In fact, I'd left home only a couple of years after I discovered those photos. With a jolt I remembered that today was my father's birthday. I did a quick calculation, and discovered that he'd be seventy. So I went out and bought a card with a car, a house, some roses on it. Inside, it said "What is a Father?" And a verse told.

EIGHTH

There were steep steps in the corner of the park I told you about earlier. I used to hop down them on one leg until I fell and broke my nose.

My first job saw me sweeping leaves and dirt near these steps. Inspecting the steps, I realized that Preston had already swept them. It didn't make much sense sweeping them again. I could make him out near the lake, his white coat splotched red from the slaughtering (something they hadn't told me about when I applied for the job).

A woman was sitting on top of the steps. I walked up the grassy slope, to approach her from behind. I leaned over and touched her directly between her legs in what was meant as a friendly gesture. To my surprise, she was friendly in response. I walked to her front, and looked at her face. It was Preston's wife. I stood confused. I knew Preston was married, and had met his wife. But his wife wasn't the woman I'd just touched. I picked up my broom again and began to sweep along the balustrade and along the terrace with its ornamental pilasters. Leaves kicked up all round. I swept the stairs again, but she was gone.

At the bottom, a number of people were dancing in a circle and burning leaves. They were humming. I went over and asked what had happened to their music. They pointed out a group to the left, repairing the machine.

I didn't want to stay where the only music was mechanical.

NINTH

I have a few disabilities. I can't, for example, open a car door. Not if I have to push that chrome bulb with my thumb. I have to ask for the door to be opened for me. I'm sick of explaining to people. They think I'm accustomed to better things and resent my presence from that moment.

The fact is, however, that my thumbs were first dislocated by my father's nephew's wife at her summer place by some lake in Alberta. She had a satyr's face, and her short stocky body was immensely strong. She had just finished jumping up and down on the trampoline for an hour after water-skiing all morning—you would never know she was an epileptic. She crept up behind me as I sat puzzling over Pierre Reverdy and got me in a double half-Nelson. I struggled to my feet but, as I tried to turn and face her, pushing her away and holding out my arms to keep her at a distance and reason with her, she grabbed my right hand in one of those fingerhooks they use in professional wrestling to bring the opponent to his knees. I thought of kicking her, but decided that would be ungentlemanly, so I struggled as best I could. I got my right hand loose but she grabbed it again by the thumb. As I tugged, the thumb popped out of its socket. Repeat the same story for another fifteen minutes and you have the story of my two dislocated digits.

But before you feel sorry for me, I have to say there is some consolation. One day I was lying on my bed, having nothing better to do. I put my thumbs on my eyes, and pushed gently (or, with injured thumbs, as hard as I was able). I hit a magic spot, a spot that maybe only delicate or maimed thumbs can reach. Just before my thumbs popped out, a vision appeared. I call it my thumb-image.

It is always the same. The face is never anyone I know, but it is as elegant as a cameo and just as clear. It stares at me, and I try to hold it for as long as possible before, as I apply too much pressure to make more happen, the thumb jars out and I leap to my feet with a yell.

From the right eye I get a woman's face: from the left, a man's. They don't know each other, that much is plain. One never looks across at where the other might be. I know neither of them, though I am familiar with every line on their almost smooth faces. All three of us are strangers and never say a word, though I sense they have known me for some time. All that's left after each encounter is pain at the roots of my thumbs.

There is something else also. While the two faces stare out in silence, a whole other scene is being played out somewhere in somebody else's head to which I have access. This scene involves a middle-aged crude-looking man and his motley gangsters. He always walks into the same ill-lit room with one bed, sits on the bed, pulls down a white phone on a long chord from the ceiling, and calls his mother. The gang grumble, mumble, ill at ease. But the boss ignores them and checks in with mamma to let her know he'll be late that evening and not to bother to try to keep the pizza hot.

Over the months, even years, it has struck me that perhaps there are various stories at the various pressures. That there is something more to know about the relationships between the two faces and myself and the gang. Are the two faces commenting on the action with their silence? Is the gangster calling someone I know? Whose head are we all living in? The more the material, and varied, the more rich connections there are to be discovered. I have only just begun the process, whose success depends on how soon I blind myself or how long my thumbs will stand up to constant abuse.

As it is, as things stand, from time to time I have thrust both thumbs into my sockets until the pain from the eyeballs was greater than the pain from the dislocations. I have blacked out the whole scene before I myself blacked out. It seems there is just one delicate pressure-point where they all live, and they exist nowhere else. The simultaneity of the faces and the action on this narrow waveband, however, does not alter the fact that we are all strangers to each other. It is I who bring them all into some sort of relation with my thumbs, and at a certain point get nothing more. Beyond that point there is just blackness and pain. Perhaps I have latched onto someone else's dream, or someone dreaming me. But I don't believe such stuff. It is my thumb-image keeps me going.

But I want to know what is beyond the blackness and the pain.

TENTH

It's not surprising I can't sleep, with my eyes hurting and people running through my head all night. Generally, though, my nights are free from outside interruption. Only the cat stirring at the foot of the bed, or a rat in the ceiling chewing on some centuries-old beam, will make me restless. And sometimes in the dead quiet I get lonely. I have lost friends this way, for I will call them when they're fast asleep.

One night I called someone. The phone made one bleep, then died. I'd been dialing O's in the dark. Then I got an operator with a black accent so heavy it was almost incomprehensible.

"Name, address, apartment number, phone number, color . . ."

"*Color?*"

"Color. What kind?"

"*Kind?* It's a black phone."

"Is it a slimline, a –"

"No, it's just a phone."

"What appears to be the trouble?"

"Incoming calls ring once then die. With outgoing, while I'm talking there's often a busy signal."

"What appears to –"

"*I just told you!*"

"A'right. Now, there's *always* only one note and always a busy signal, huh?"

"*No.* Only sometimes."

"Uhu," she says, "only *sometimes* it rings once and –"

"No!" I yell. "Always!"

"So it *always* just rings once and there's a busy signal, right?"

"No. *No! Sometimes* a busy signal on *outgoing*. Not always. Always is the incoming."

"Oh," she says. "Always only one ring and sometimes a busy signal—but maybe someone's talking. Maybe the line's busy."

"No," say I. "I just said *I'm* talking. To the person."

"Then how can the line be busy?" she inquires.

"It's *not*," I whisper. "But in the background there's a signal."

She gives up.

"Can you be reached at another number?"

"No," I reply. "I've only got one phone. This one. No slimline. Just a phone."

"OK," she says. "I'll call you back in fifteen minutes."

I get up and go to the bathroom. I say to myself: "You watch. I'll sit down and the phone will ring." It does. She says:

"They'll send a repairman between nine and five."

I replied that I couldn't stay in all day.

"Why not?" she wants to know.

"Why not? Well, like millions of others I have to work."

"So how can we repair the phone? We can't just send out repairmen like that."

"Give me a time. Call before the man sets out. Give me a time."

"We can't do that," she says.

"How about between nine and twelve," I ask.

"Alrighty," she says.

And then the phone exploded in my ear, and a recording said: "This is a recording. There appears to be something wrong with your phone." I jammed it down. Immediately it rang.

"Who is it?" I asked. "*Who?* I can't hear. Call back," I yelled, dropping the phone onto its cradle. It rang again.

There was a clear click and a clear voice.

"Is Eli Passum there?"

"Wrong number!" I yelled.

The phone sat in its bed. Then it rang again.

Someone else's line.

I listened for hours.

~

Those were the clear days that brought cleansing winds from Canada. I dreaded them. The chimney of the nearby garbage-burner swirled its smoke down on me, and the cold north wind became poisoner not purifier. My eyes got filled with grit. Minute particles of unburnt garbage lodged under my contact lenses and even though I had evolved techniques for dislodging the muck, my eye ached all day.

One day I'd had enough. I picked up the phone and called Allen D. Dorp. Commissioner, The City of New York, Department of Air Resources, 120 Wall Street, New York, NY 10015. Telephone number (212). 482. 6230. (He'd given me his card with its gold crest at a New Year party and encouraged me to call). I'd called before. This time, however, he was in. He must have misheard the name and thought it was somebody from City Hall. I told him my complaint.

"Does it happen all the time?" he asked, dully I thought.

"No," I said, "only on the clear days that bring cleansing winds from Canada."

"In this case," he replied, "there's nothing we can do. It's an act of God."

And hung up.

~

Days of continuous rain had leached the piles of dog shit, or washed them away. One turd lay at my feet, split open, soft parts eroded, the gritty parts left. A teeshirt walked by saying "Goodnight Vienna." Two gays dressed identically in white undershirts and tight jeans lilted by. A sportscar with its back plastic window cracked, torn, and taped flung itself past. And I passed a woman I didn't know. "I'm growing mildew under my armpits," I said. My legs felt dizzy, my throat tight. 514. 2301. I'd called from home and then from three boxes. I'd promised to call that morning, but storms and nightmares had kept me awake and exhausted, and I hadn't woken till one p.m. to no light and no time. Then, when I called, the phone was busy till 2. I'd called the phone company who'd rung with the same results. They refused to verify, however, since the day was Sunday. She'd said she had made bread, and was saving me a loaf. I went to the gym.

I pushed the button for the elevator. The doors opened. I stepped inside and pushed 5. No light went on. Doors closed. Nothing. I pushed again. Nothing. Anxious, I pushed all the buttons at random, hoping to shake something loose. The doors opened. I went back out. Steam rose from the streets. Faces passed. I noted details as a way of holding onto them. Hair, nose, eyes. Keys, bicycle, family group with baby. I felt I was floating. I tried the phone again. Nothing. As soon as I could I tried again. The busy signal had stopped, but now only empty ringings echoed in my ear. A siren blew off. A red engine crashed by. An ambulance. The empty ringing was obliterated. I pocketed my dime. My legs were somewhere beneath me. I was all in parts. My head was flying off. Even if she'd been in I wouldn't have known what to say. When I was with her I was on edge and looked forward to her leaving. When she left I was on edge and felt deprived. Why hadn't she called? She mustn't care as much as she seemed. And that was fine. Got me off the hook. If that was how she wanted it. But she should have called. I could have been dead for all she knew. I'd asked her to go away with me for a week. Then I remembered she'd asked me the same thing, and I'd said no. Said I couldn't stand bus journeys.

I must be dead. That was the only logical explanation. Or asleep. The dead idea seemed the more likely. Nobody looked at me, so I mustn't be there. Nobody talked to me so they couldn't see me. I pushed into a group on the sidewalk and went right through like a hot knife. I called again. Busy. Silence. I went home. I used my keys with my eyes closed. By rote. I opened the door to my basement apartment. Since I was dead, maybe the cat I loved would be there waiting behind the door. Maybe he would greet me as he always had with joy and love and rush down the stairs ahead of me, his tail high, his little black button leading on, kindly light. I would hug the cat for five minutes as I always had until the cat was ready to be put down, when he'd run for the food place, and eat. I kept my eyes closed. Death could bring some reward. But there was no cat.

I didn't care if I fell down the stairs or not. I scarcely felt the crack my head received from the wall at the bottom. I blundered about, eyes closed tight, hoping still to meet some of the loved dead. The stable dead. All the lines were down in the storm. Silence lay all over the city. Confusing busy lying signals. Everybody dead. Goodnight Vienna. In the dark basement with its heavy velvet curtains permanently drawn, the phone rang. When I opened my eyes everything was as dark as inside my lids. A table was on its side, books strewn. A glass lay shattered with a vase beside it. The record player lay smashed on the carpet. My eyes grew used to the dark gradually, and I saw the ringing. It got brighter. I sat down on the floor among the broken objects and put my hands over my eyes.

ELEVENTH

For months I have had this headache: from window to window. It comes from the twisting of ropes, from the constant banging on the walls, from the screech of worn tires, from the flushing of a toilet every time a door slams. I have this headache from coast to coast, deriving from the slam of waves on the beaches, the lancing of so many rivers, the gaffing of so many gulls, the colliding of clouds and the blaring of suns. I have this headache from pole to pole, from the scraping of moles and the tunnelling of earthworms. The breathing of crickets has set my teeth on edge, and the blinking of frogs. Is there no anodyne or panacea? Must I block my ears with sand and crawl off to imagine silence? And what if it is only my imagination that is at fault? What if there is nothing out there to have a silence, or is capable of silence? And what if inside silence itself is the absolute obverse of this din, deafening in its aphony, a mirror cacophonic nothing? What if, in the mute hush, the blood in the ear talks back? It is a fly in the ear, sending you mad. You are now afraid to take your fingers out of your ears, and afraid to put them in. Or what if inside silence is a constant maddening whirr, like charged particles inside an atom?

You wish that you had never been born, or that the end of the world had come simply and definitively, with a clear distinction between noise and silence, life and death.

You wish. But nothing changes.

~

After such a reverie I find myself sitting here. He faces me. I am looking at him. Every move I make is not so much recorded as imitated. The man is doing what I am doing, but with minute variations, and a split second after. We are not simultaneous, but our aims are alike. I move slowly, giving him a chance to adapt, even get there ahead of me, but he is never willing to take the risk. He looks at me with eyes I have never seen before. If I leave and return the expression on his face has changed, not for the better. I recognize his furniture. I recognize his clothes. I wonder if he too registers recognition. I wonder if I recognize the face in the frame. I wonder if he wonders if he recognizes the face.

~

At her request, "Touch my finger," I laid down this feeling as law: Never probe what is outside you. Consequently the moment passed, and the request was never made again.

The only mystery still attaching to this anecdote, in my mind at least, was why it was assumed by the other at the very beginning that a touch of one finger acting on another guaranteed the possibilities of psychic change. In my experience, psychic change occurred when least expected, if at all. And then, while I was thinking about this, the less cynical I became because I remembered something that had changed my life a little, even though I was responsible for its creation (does it matter where change comes from, so long as it comes?)

I was given a piece of folded paper, or cardboard bent in two. Then she left. On it were all the cells, seeds, eggs, organisms, that would recreate life. But only if it was left out in the rain.

I took it into the back yard and laid it in the heavy red dust that had settled everywhere. I pushed back into the house through the wire-screen, and sat looking up at the sky.

Blue. Blue. Blue.

I sat a long time.

I had almost given up when the clouds suddenly banked and the sky went slate. The heavens opened. I looked out the back door, down the steps. Water was rising. I calculated that two more steps and I'd be flooded. I waited for life to begin. I could see the paper nowhere. The water was rising. I opened the door again. The water was rising.

~

On the log I placed the plastic cup with its contents: the avocado seed that had failed to fertilize, despite being talked to. The toothpicks I used to keep it from falling into the water still stuck out like contact detectors on a mine. The cup collapsed slowing without catching fire. The seed lay there, being enclosed in hot ice. It was so waterlogged it would not burn. Its own fire of decay kept it intact. The log was eaten away. Then the faint smell of scorched plastic blew away. The avocado seed dried out slowly, encased and shining in its glass bed, fallen into the ashes, good as new.

TWELFTH

About 1960 I was on vacation in England. Actually, it wasn't really a vacation. I was thinking of setting up a fish and chips chain across the States. If my project had worked out I would have been a millionaire by now, anticipating Arthur Treacher.

One experience in particular gave me food for thought. I had only been in the country a day or two, and one evening was walking round Tottenham when I smelled the familiar smell. I waited outside the shop till it opened, and I was first in. Huge vats of boiling fat were bubbling, and in them were the wire-net baskets full of frying potatoes. But I could see no fish in the fat, and none draining through the holes in the metal shelf at the back, being kept hot. As I stood waiting to be asked what I wanted, the man in charge bent down beneath the counter and pulled on what seemed to be an old carpet. He heaved the beast head first into the fat. The body trailed over the edge, but the head began to sizzle. Hairs came out of the muzzle and floated, frying to a crisp. Bubbles encased teeth and gums.

"Excuse me," I said to the man, "But do you have any fish? Cod? Plaice?"

"Fish?" the man repeated, cutting an uncooked flank steak.

"Fish? No fish tonight, mate. Or any other night. Not that much around anymore. It's ass tonight. Fish in a month, maybe. Ass and chips. Want a nice piece of ass with your chips, then?"

He could see I was disappointed. I just didn't think this would go over big in the States, and despaired of ever becoming a millionaire.

THIRTEENTH

I was spending a quiet night at home watching TV, "Scenes from the Revolution."

There were awful scenes of violence, all in great detail. Someone was being held down in the middle of a circle, and old men were beating up on him or her. I could see the head bobbing from the blows. Somewhere else, men in thick glasses were beating up someone else who was being held, arms pinioned. These scenes, and variations, were continually repeated, and it became clear that most of those being beaten were women. I sat staring at the screen.

There was a general in the room with me, a general I'd met on the volleyball court at Washington Square Park. There were a few other people too, but I didn't know them. The general didn't have a TV, and had asked if he could come over to see the program, to see who had aided and who had opposed the Revolution.

It was clear to see that the Revolutionaries had been doing most of the beating, if not all. A frenzied man chased a woman across the screen again and again. He stabbed the air with a long knife. I felt I had to say something.

"You must know," I began, "that although I'm not a woman, when the Revolution first began I went to an outdoor rally in Miami. I tried to choose sides, but I got very confused. The women, who were the oppressed, refused to join the Revolution. The men, who were the oppressors, were the Revolutionaries."

"In other words," said the general, stroking the thick gold braid all down the front of his jacket, and feeling for something in his pocket, "you are against the Revolution . . ."

FOURTEENTH

I have told you how I spent my childhood and adolescence in England. And I told you I have been back since. There was one place (I won't say where in case it is flooded with tourists), which I used to visit again and again. It was where I had my first mystical experience (I have been plagued with them since), as part of one of the eight choirs used in the Gabrieli 40-part motet "Spem in Alium."

I went back to the place one summer in my twenties, having tried a number of jobs in the U.S. and succeeded in none. So I tried G.B. with similar results. I felt my failure was not for lack of trying, but for lack of not trying. I used to work so hard my fellow-workmen would gang up. "You're spoiling it for the rest of us," they'd complain, just before ostracizing me—what the English call 'being sent to Coventry'. Well, I went back to where I'd first seen some meaning in life that I couldn't comprehend and which made me think I wasn't living where I thought I was living; "where modes of being intersected."

From outside, I could see that the gorgeous Renaissance Chapel roof had been burnt recently, but had just been repaired. It was brighter than the rest of the building, and the renovation had been done in a modern style, one, it seemed to me, that hadn't been invented yet. I went in and wandered around the rich-smelling gloom. I sidled over to the staircase in the corner that only those in the know used, and that only seldom since the stairs were so steep and went so high. Up I climbed, squeezed and getting very tired, until I came to the huge space between the chapel ceiling and the real roof, an attic or loft that ran the half-mile length of the building. It was here, years ago, I'd seen the signatures left by the medieval stone masons, left where few men would ever see them, but where God would always be able to see them at a glance (if he could see through the lead-coated roof itself).

I heard a noise, and went towards it. A young man, about my age, was sitting astride a beam, carving wood parts and figures. He held his instruments between his knees and was working away, totally concentrated, absolutely alone. All the time he was looking at his work as it existed in a mirror. He never looked directly at his work.

FIFTEENTH

Work seems to be good ways of enlarging one's horizons. I recently took a job as a temporary medical orderly. My big chance came when I had to stand in for the regular doctor. My first patient, and my last so far, was a thirty-five year-old man, married, father of three and guardian of four, who came in with neurodermatitis. That is, the skin on his head was falling off and he was getting a thing about it. Small wonder. He looked awful. He told me he kept dreaming of mixing cement. Small wonder he had dermatitis.

Then he told me he didn't know how to mix cement. What kind of a man is it doesn't know how to mix cement? I was mixing cement for my father's path through the garden at 7. At 8 I was breaking bricks for my grandfather's path. I had to play both sides. Don't tell me about neurodermatitis.

And then he told me his house needed tuckpointing. What am I, a tuckpointer? Tuckpointing. I'm supposed to know what tuckpointing is. How could I possibly have helped the guy if he used such language? I told him to go back and dream that his house needed painting instead. Tuckpointing . . .

When he returned, he told me he had *hired* someone to mix the cement. He forgot about the painting as soon as I said it. Typical. I don't know how they survive. All houses need painting at least once every three years, unless you're by the sea. In which case you should do it as often as you can afford. And he told me his wife went to a bingo game. What do I care about his wife?

The last time I saw him he apologized for being late. He'd had to take care of the kids, he said; put them to bed and then wait for the wife to come home. He hadn't been able to get to his night job. Then came the lie I'd been waiting for, and which I'd been trained to look out for. He said he was a hit and run driver who'd killed a child. He didn't understand how everyone had been able to leave the scene, but everybody had. So there were no witnesses. So, he said, he didn't exist.

Well, there was no point in telling the poor devil that he didn't depend on his dreams for his existence. He *did* depend on them, and lived through them. They were the mirrors to the most significant side of his existence. There were no such significant mirrors on this daily side. He preferred to be certain. On *this* side is just guesswork. I sat with him, guessing.

Then I asked him to leave, and went out to do some shopping. I also wanted to drop in at a bank close by which had always looked attractive from the outside.

I opened the door, walked in, and sat down at the nearest empty desk. I picked up a Savings Certificate Agreement and improved its wording with a fancy pen that was lying beside a pack of menthol cigarettes. It now read: "PENALTIES FOR PREMATURE WITHDRAWAL. The owner may not withdraw without consent. If a withdrawal is made without consent the owner will receive a reduced rate."

I looked up. The young blue-suited official with his own desk nearby was filling out forms. The fountain behind him under the clock spouted real water over unreal toads. On his desk sat a limp miniature Old Glory. Set neatly to its right was a galleon in full sail, and off in the corner near the window was a Red Indian smoking a calumet and wearing a head-dress with feathers tipped toothpaste pink. Over his head was a diploma, framed. My eye came back to the desk with its tiny herbivarium, neat and round. It went well with the selection of "My Fair Lady" which the organist was playing.

The young woman came back to her desk. Small tits, no bra. The nipples poked through the blouse. When she sat down and turned her back to me, I could see the strap. So there was a bra . . . She hitched her striped blue and white pants, turned, and twitched her thin-crack lips.

"Yes?"

It came out "yis?"

"What can I do for you?"

I scrunched up the Savings Certificate Agreement.

"I want to deposit this plant."

I held out the spider-plant cutting in the sandwich bag, the cutting I'd snipped from its parent in the doctor's office.

"Yis," she said, not looking up from the papers, paperback novel, pack of menthol cigarettes for women, chains of paperclips.

"For how long?"

"Perpetuity," I replied. "If possible."

Almost before I'd finished she'd made out the forms.

"Sign here please. And here. It's 6.55% on term deposits which mature one year or more after the date on deposit credit."

I stood up, gathering my sandwich bag to me.

"I've changed my mind. I think I'll spend the plant instead."

As I left, the organist was playing "The Way We Were."

I have had no word from my place of work for some time. Perhaps the doctor is still on holiday. But I have not been wasting my time. I have been spending it well, and improving my mind with famous people who come to visit me from time to time. The latest person who dropped in was—well, I can't give you his name. He's *that* famous. But I can tell you he chain-smoked from the moment he arrived to the moment he left.

SIXTEENTH

I can't, personally, vouch for the truth of this story, but it was reported to me by a friend who has always seemed to me a truthful person (I can't tell you his name because he is still alive, and there may be repercussions). I'm retelling the story now because it says something important about the state of the arts today (or as it was a few years back—but I have no reason to believe things have changed all that much).

Some intimates of a famous painter wanted to take a new friend to meet him. Not finding him in his studio, they went up to the high glass attic to see if he was there. They pushed open the trapdoor. Birds, pigeon-size and smaller, hopped about in many cages. There was a peculiar smell and a good deal of noise. The painter called from the pile of sunlight at the far corner, welcoming them. They walked over.

"I painted all of these birds, you know," said the painter, to the new friend in particular. "I paint them in two different colors; one side one color-striped, the other colors of a different stripe—birds of a different stripe." He laughed. Then, walking over to a cage, he reached inside and grabbed a bird by the neck. He swung it round and round until it snapped, and hung limp from his fingers. The visitor turned and left, but the painter followed close behind, asking him to wait and see what else he could do.

"Look!" he called. "Look, I'm picking out its guts with my nails now. Look!"

SEVENTEENTH

The following story, however, I can vouch for, since I was there. The artist is not the same fellow we met in the previous chapter, but I believe they are related. The state of the arts today seems to me just about hopeless if these two people are typical of the profession, as I believe they are.

One day I went to visit this artist in the hope that he'd have some work for me to do, some modelling, for instance—I'm a bit barrel-chested and short-legged, but then so was Odysseus, my classical friends tell me. This artist, however, was more interested in my hands, which he had used in a number of his sculptures (though what he transformed them into were something as different from hands as I am from Lana Turner). I have delicate unspoiled hands.

As I entered his studio, I noticed the large brass statue of a man standing in a corner in front of the large coffin-shaped acid-bath in which he had been made. The artist was explaining part of the process loudly to no one in particular, all the time stirring a substance into the sides of a lethal-looking hot liquid with a kind of spatula to keep it flowing and prevent it sticking. I wondered about where the stuff went when he'd finished with it. The sewers? He read my thoughts. "Sometimes it gets backed up as far as Elizabeth. Pockets form. So you have to stir this in."

We moved to another room. I was plucking up courage to ask him if he had any work for me, and hoping he'd read my mind so I wouldn't have to ask. But the artist was more preoccupied than ever today. There was another huge tub in the middle of the room. He stepped into it, carrying with him two of his latest creations which had large inflatable red chests, like frigate birds. The chests were slack just then, but the artist squeezed something in his right hand and the chests billowed out. The two things started splashing him. I wondered what would happen if the artist got the acid in his eyes, but he didn't seem to be in any danger.

I suddenly realized that what was going on was a *performance*, in a room that altered before my eyes. It became large as a swimming pool, huge as an auditorium. I looked up and saw spectators in a high gallery near the roof. Over the public address came the announcement that after the performance of avant-garde sculpting there would be a discussion on who was the real realist, Raphael or Jasper Johns. A discussion on the changing concepts of realism would follow that.

So much for my hands.

EIGHTEENTH

I am now, as in all good autobiographies, going to let you in on my home life. It is still rather less than easy in my mind, so I am telling it, at least to start with, in the third person. That way I can pretend it happened to someone else, and the sympathy I feel for the character will be anonymous or abstract. I will be able to read about it all and then lay down the book and go about my business, little affected, as though it was just another book that I was reading.

It is a fact that every time I return I swear never to go back. But back I go. And each time my visits are weird. It's gotten so that I'm not even sure it's home I'm returning to, and I seem stuck in a certain time-groove. I don't seem adult. I seem to be looking at an old film, with a man standing in front of a jasmine bush newly in bloom, trained against the newly-whitewashed garden wall. His mo-ped has its handlebars in the bush, and the motor is still sputtering. An adolescent boy runs through the kitchen and out onto the narrow path of broken bricks. "Clear the hell out!" he calls. "What the hell do you think you're doing? You think this is a main road or something?"

The man smiles and takes off his plaid cap.

"Excuse," he says in a foreign accent, "but I seem to have lost my way. Does Henri live here?"

"Henry? Henry who? What the hell are you up to, mister? There's no Henry here, and this is *our* path."

"Oh, then, my mistake! A thousand pardons!"

And he puts on his hat, gives a little precise hitch to his plus-fours, extricates the handlebars, turns his machine round, and revs up the small motor mounted on the back.

"A thousand apologies!" he calls again, as he starts to bowl slowly down the garden path which the boy had made with his father.

The boy stands watching. Then he sees a branch recently sawed off the old pear tree, picks it up, and swings at the man with the dead wood. The rotten branch just misses the back wheel and breaks off in his hands. The boy becomes doubly angry. He takes off after the man, throwing after him the piece of wood that has remained in his hands. Stooping to pick up some other dead wood, he chases the man down the garden, past the asbestos garage his father and he himself had erected. He dashes out through the open creosoted gate, out into the lane. The man on the bike wards off the blows, smiling good-naturedly, and all the time miraculously keeping his balance with one hand, and sometimes with no hands at all. His moustache gleams with pomade in the sun. When he gets well into the lane he revs up the engine again, for it has conked out. He helps it out with a thrust or two of his legs in the gravel, then kicks hard on the pedals. He moves off in a little whirlwind of dust and gravel and small puffs of smoke. The boy stops and stares after him, wondering how the man had gotten into the garden in the first place. He and his father had rigged up a latch at the top of the six-foot gate, to open which you had to know exactly where to reach, and be able to stretch quite some distance over the top and down a ways.

As he stands, thinking, a group of three or four businessmen come by. This part of town is not where they live, gather, or work. And they are wearing bowler hats. They pass him, but keep looking back over their shoulders. Eventually, one of the men comes back and takes the boy aside. He is very polite, but there is something like unuttered outrage in his voice.

"I say, sonny, what *are* you doing? Do you know who that is?"

"What's it to you? I don't care who he is. Nobody comes riding up my path asking for Henry. He got what he deserves."

"Well," continues the man, "I'll tell you who that was. Just for your information, that was—"

The boy hears some name, but by that time the man has walked away. The gate has closed behind him, but the boy reaches over the top for the familiar mechanism, snicks the button, and gives the door into his special garden a good kick with his foot. He walks back slowly. To his left, rows of plants, leaves the shape of tobacco or milkweed but with the variegated colors of coleus, are planted row after row. A new strain of something like lettuce which his father is trying out. His mother sticks her head out of the kitchen door.

"Dinner!" she calls.

Light shines into the kitchen, which is rather cluttered but cozy. The boy and his sister are sitting at rightangles to each other round a small square table. The experimental vegetable sits in side-dishes, and the main course of something good and brown sits in front of each. In the middle of the table is something large and decorated with brilliant patterns and colors. It is shaped like an egg, like a Ukranian Easter egg, the boy thinks.

"What's that?" he asks his mother, pointing.

"Boiled egg," she replies. "What's it look like?"

"Who was that man you beat today?" his sister asks.

She is overweight, and generally the boy doesn't pay too much attention to her. She also told tales on him and got him into trouble.

"Somebody. Who knows?"

"But what was his name?"

"*Jesus!* How do I know his name!"

"Ma!—"

"Shut up! It was some foreign name. One of the men round back told me. One Grease. One something."

"One Grease? What's he? A mechanic? He selling them bikes or something?"

"How the hell— "

"Oh, you swore! Ma— "

"*Jesus!* He's not a grease monkey. He's a famous painter or something. And I don't know what kind of painter, before you ask. Maybe a house-painter."

"Oh, now I remember!" she almost yells, technicolor vegetable sticking between her braced front teeth.

"It's not One Grease. It's *Juan Gris!* He's *famous!* Why aren't you famous yet? You're always saying— "

"Who's that?" the boy interrupts.

His father has just come in, a canvas wrapped in newspaper under one arm, and hanging from the other a young woman. He brings her in and sits her down. They are smiling at each other. The boy's mother makes her comfortable.

" 'Nude With Still Life' he painted," his sister calls out. "Or the other way round, 'Still Life With Nude'. I saw it in a book in school, in the library. There was a violin somewhere."

"Who's that?" the boy asks again, quietly, as his father and the young woman caress each other, ignoring him, ignoring everybody. His mother and sister seem to see nothing. "How did she get in *here?*" he repeated, but nobody is listening to him. He pushes his chair away from the table slowly, beginning to feel overwhelmed by a feeling of great melancholy.

NINETEENTH

The years were eaten in silence. The son ate his father's green eyes with the speck of cinder in the left iris. He ate his mother's mildness and devious ways of keeping the peace. He ate his sister for not being somebody else. He swallowed it all without chewing, gristle and fat, holding his breath to avoid the taste. He was a silent eater, though his father accused him of making noises when he chewed. He hardly ever chewed. He grew thin and left home. He left home for many years with the sound of his father's jaws in his ears, the speck of grit in cold jade in his eyes, still on his lips the crumbs of his mother's peace-lies. His sister's confusion slipped down his spine and hampered his feet, for it was his own confusion. In her he saw himself.

In foreign lands he ate noisily. He put on fat. Since the talk at home had been money, he earned enough money not to consider himself too much of a failure, though it confused him, and he stayed clear of commitment. He did not want to own or be owned.

When he felt his limbs knit firmer and his muscles pull themselves together, and when there was money in his hands, he decided to return to his country, even though he no longer regarded it as his own. There was fear in his bones.

He told his father about his successes, his plans, his ideals. They ate in silence. The father was eating too noisily to notice any changes.

"There's some fellow from the office going over there for six months. They're giving him twenty thousand."

The son realized that whatever he did would provide no more than a snack for his father. He shrank into his plate.

"I cannot get money out of here to live where I want. The Communist government we have has restrictions on everything. That's where I thought you'd come in useful. Now I see you won't."

And still the son tried to accommodate himself to his father's needs and interests, as he always had done. He talked of steam locomotives and roses; of sex and fertilizer; of money. To ingratiate himself further, he said: "I can't decide if I want to stay a citizen of this country. I want to know if I can get a pension here more than there, or there more than here, or whether they'd cut off my pension in one or the other place, or how much I get single or married. I'm very worried about my pension." His father said: That's how I like to see you thinking. And almost touched him.

And the son poured boiling water over himself, and sliced his tongue with the bread-knife.

After his parents had fallen asleep over television, he crawled upstairs to the childhood bed where his feet stuck out the end. The blankets, that summer night, were so tightly tucked in, and the comforter so heavy, that he almost stifled. Stripping the bed quietly, he lay down on the bare springs.

Next morning they were walking in the garden. The son had just, at his father's request, climbed up to the old barrel which the previous owner of the house had wedged many years ago into the fork of a great elm. It used to house doves. But the doves had flown off soon after their installation, or had been eaten by rats. The father said that squirrels occupied the barrel now and then, and he wanted to keep them away from his garden, where they tugged up the grass and rummaged among his bulbs. The son was in the garage, putting away the ladder, when he heard his father:

"Look at that! What do you make of that! Damn and blast!" The son looked over to where his father was down on his knees by the open gate as if praying. Two symmetrical lines of geraniums lined the driveway. Between the two rows at regular intervals were rhododendron cuttings. One geranium lay on its side, its stem snapped off. The earth around had been dug and scattered. The father brought down curses on the dog, and was incapacitated from action by fury. He seemed as upset by the disruption of symmetry as by the deed of wanton destruction. The son went over and suggested that they put the broken stem in a pot with special soil for cuttings. It might take again. He also suggested that one of the plants growing in a reserve bed near the front door might be brought up to replace the deceased. This was done, possibly because the son went on to point out that the action would lead to an increase in order and symmetry: the flowers near the broken plant were all in a more advanced state of bloom than the dead plant, which had been rather backward. The son indicated the reserve plants. "They look very healthy there, even though they're so close together."

"So they ought to be healthy," his father replied.

"There's good manure under the roots. Every time I shoot a squirrel I bury it there. I'd like to put that dog alongside them."

And his mother had told him his father only used his gun to frighten the squirrels away.

"What's those lumps in the soil?" the son asked, as he turned away. He knew he ought to begin the ritual admiration of the roses. To put off that moment he asked about the soil.

"That's shit. Human shit. They give it to you free, and you just pay for delivery. They brought it in a lorry and dumped it in the driveway. I spent two days in it up to my armpits. And nobody was here to help me. I could have done with some help. Especially picking out those condoms."

The son flushed.

"Why are you growing those roses so high?" he asked.

"They're almost as tall as that pine I planted years ago."

"To stop people looking in," was the reply. "I'm preparing the fence back there with barbed wire for roses to climb on."

"Why not simply build a twenty-foot fence all round, with a drawbridge. That would keep the dogs out too."

"Not a bad idea," said the father.

They moved toward the garage, and the son knew it was time to admire whatever the father was growing on the roof by some ingenious method or other. He reflected that he was glad that this time he didn't have a woman with him. Once, his father had persuaded him to climb up the ladder first, and then the woman. He realized too late that his father's insistence was not out of politeness, but in order to have him out of the way while he stared up the woman's dress. The extra insult was to have had his father leer at him as if he were also in on the conspiracy.

This time it was tomatoes grown under plastic. "What makes them grow so well," the son inquired, politely.

"Blood. Dried blood. Here's one ready. Take it down."

The son counted the days that made up his duty. He held his breath for the remainder. Poured hot blood over himself, then hot dung.

There was a great drought in the fenland. The black fens were going up in clouds. Restrained by no trees, the rich peat was clogging the remaining watercourses and blocking lungs. Farmers were ploughing back their rootcrops that hadn't fertilized. They were letting their animals graze the wheat fields and barley. Ten farmers hanged themselves in one week as they plunged heavier into debt, for this was but the latest in a series of dry years.

It was near his parents' 35th wedding anniversary. At silent dinner he asked if he could take them out to supper later in the week. His father stopped chewing, sat back, and said:

"If you had money I'd be delighted. But here you are, wandering around by the cheapest ways possible, travelling on a shoestring and cutting corners. To tell the truth—let me speak out—" (the mother collapsed into her mild protest), "I'd feel guilty spending your money. When we visited your cousin in Canada we were feted—"

"But that's different!" his wife interjected. "He's a millionaire, and it's all different now, and his wife's divorced him and taken—"

"Yes, I know all that! And kindly let me speak, will you? I don't expect *that*, but I do expect you to have a place of your own by now. At 24 it was alright. But how old are you now? 34? And what'll you be at 44?"

"The same as now, I hope," the son mumbled.

"I hope!" echoed the father. "If you had a place of your own and property there's nothing I'd like better than to have you take us out. But with what you earn—I tell you, I don't approve of your life. I don't approve at all!"

There was something prehistoric about his father. Nothing could lighten the cave. The son sat silent and could eat no more. He sat silent, clamped in childhood. He was ten years old, the age when he had first seen his father and grown to prefer an uncle, a fact that didn't escape the father with his one fascinating frightening eye. The son felt terror and panic rising. Terrified of the vision of future misery and present inadequacy which his father had conjured up again now, as he had in the past, continually. Often the son forgot his man's bulk and felt himself vulnerable, small, somehow ridiculous and ugly to look at. He was terrified of being on the streets when this happened. As he sat at table, silence all round, he was unable to move. He grew terrified of his own hatred for himself, and of his father, and of his contempt for his mother. He was ashamed of what he had let his father do to his mother, and angry at his helplessness, angry that he still kept trying to win approval from the man.

He could hardly breathe. With an effort, he pushed himself away from the table. He rose quietly. It was time to leave again.

He poured boiling pitch upon the house and its inhabitants.

He knew he'd be back, to sort through the wreckage.

TWENTIETH

And back I went one year, not having any particular desire to go anywhere, but with three weeks sick leave owed me in NJ. Instead of going straight to my father's house, however, I went to the farm where I used to help out as a child—picking rhubarb, putting cardboard tops on the milkbottles in the dairy which always smelled milk-greasy, and where cold water always ran down the wall and along a small trough, even in summer . . .

But when I arrived where the farm used to be, it was not there. The whole area had been modernized. The village green where the cows used to pause for a last tuft of grass before their nightly milking was now a playing field. Signs told just what kind of games could be played, and which were forbidden. Concrete paths made diagonal crossings, and on the site of the farm was a home for old people, neat little bungalows with tidy front gardens and tidy senior citizens.

I took the train to my father's house. The weather was unusually balmy when I arrived, so we went for a walk along the path that led down to the valley. We came to the hut where the kids used to hang out.

"That's now a bus station," my father said. "Or rather, a passenger shelter where they can wait for the long-distance buses. And there's the rose-bush."

I looked across the field. There was the bush with its huge white roses and the scent I'd never forgotten. It hung over another hut.

"They transplanted it. It got in the way of the buses. And look, the pigs are still there."

I looked where my father pointed, lower down the field. A whole area had been transformed into something like a yellow riverbank. Pigs lolled around in liquid mud like hippos.

"Pigs can't sweat," my father explained. "That's their only way of keeping cool."

"I know," I replied, somewhat irritated.

"And they always like the same place. They like the same mudhole. They always come back to the same muckhole."

He gave me a significant glance. The sun was dropping down.

"Let's take a car-ride," my father suggested.

I remembered his car, but agreed.

I sat in the passenger's seat. After a while I said:

"Look, I know what these leaves mean to you, but they must have been here since last year. They're not draining through the hole you drilled. My feet are starting to soak through. And they smell. Can't we throw them out?"

For a while my father said nothing. Then he stopped the car.

"Alright. Throw them out. But when the time comes you're to come back and get them. You know how important they are for compost."

I knew. I agreed. I scooped the stinking mass onto the side of the road with my bare hands.

"The car's an old Rover, you know," my father added.

"It has a right-hand drive."

Had he gone crazy?

"I know," I said, and closed my eyes.

When we got back home, I said:

"Listen, I want to go and see Johnny Woodgate."

"Johnny Woodgate?" my father replied. "He's— "

"I don't care," I said. "I want to go and see him. Where does he live?"

"Live? But he's— "

"I'll be back for supper maybe," I called out, leaving, irritated again.

The house was large. It had a high wooden fence. A hedge had separated the house from the farmyard. In this farmyard I had first seen a bull serving a cow, and a goose being killed by placing a rake over its neck, and the handle stepped on. I hadn't been inside the house often, and then only into the kitchen. Johnny Woodgate (Johnny Long as he was sometimes called, since he married old Mr. Long's daughter, and Mr. Long still owned the farm), was happy to see me. Johnny was dressed very elegantly, not at all how he used to dress. His clothes seemed somehow out of the nineteenth century. He had on a black suit and a high white collar. When I knew him and worked with him he never used to take off his high boots that were always steeped in manure, and he always seemed to wear the same greasy-looking stained riding breeches. I used to like Johnny Woodgate a lot, if only because he used to let me drive his milk-float, pulled by the gray Toby. Johnny used to let you do what you could do. He never yelled at you. As I stood looking at Johnny, it occurred to me that I loved him.

"It's been a long time," he said. "A very long time."

"Well, you're certainly elegant," I replied. "You've certainly come up in the world."

"Oh, ay," he grinned. "But clothes are nothing. It's what's inside that counts. Come, let me show you my collection of glass leaves. No falling off trees for them any more!"

The grin startled me, and his general boyishness. Johnny Woodgate had never grinned, or even smiled. He was always busy. Kind, but busy. I couldn't remember Johnny ever having said that much to me, either. Busy, that was the word. Always doing something interesting. I remembered when he first let me feed the pigs with him. I'd been terrified as we walked down the aisle between the sties. Boars reared up on hind legs, long sharp jaws inches from my body, little wicked eyes wickeder for their white lashes. Someone had told me that pigs would wait for ever if they wanted to injure you; that they could take an arm of with one bite. So I had stuck close to Johnny, so close I could even smell his dirty brown corduroy breeches.

"Do you want to see it?"

I was jolted out of my reverie.

"See it?"

"It! The collection!"

"Oh, yes! Glass leaves."

"Glass leaves on glass plants. A lost art. Almost a dead art."

I was ushered onto a balcony overlooking a large room with dark wood panelling. The balcony was filled with glass plants with glass leaves. As my feet trod on the oak plank floor, the glass leaves sang and set up a shimmer. The stems bent a little, humming. I stopped to look closer, but just then a light woman's step set up a counter-rhythm. I looked up. She was young still, slim, sharp-featured. I never remembered her like this. In a certain state of embarrassment at her gaze, I dropped my eyes. They came to rest on a glass stem with a chipped gold band. It looked very old. Mrs. Johnny Woodgate waited. I walked over to her and kissed her on both cheeks. Too late, I realized that I'd put two glass leaves in my mouth. Confused, I spat them out delicately onto my hand. But one was broken, and had cut my tongue. Red in the face, I began to explain that her husband had given them to me, but she looked away. I began again:

"How is your daughter?"

Her name was Marion, and she was a cripple, the only cripple I had known as a child. They said she had been born like that. She never joined our games, and so I hardly knew her. But she was always on the farm. I thought she must have been very delicate because she had features like the doll my mother had brought back from Holland when she was a girl.

I identified this doll with an aunt who had been captured by the Nazis a week after she married my uncle. The doll had eyelids that fluttered and eyes that closed. Her cheeks were dawn-pink and porcelain. The aunt had been tortured and killed.

"We never had a daughter. Do you think we are the Woodgates?"

I came to myself again.

"The Woodgates? Why yes! That is, I—"

"The Woodgates were my father's tenants. We had a letter this morning which might have been from him, if—"

"Let me see it!"

I heard my own rude voice, and was shocked. I tried to smile by way of apology. I began to read the letter she handed me from her dress pocket.

"Marion has just died," she said.

A sadness such as I'd never felt settled over me. I knew I would never recover my spirits. And I had so long to live.

~

I needed comfort, and familiarity. So I went by bus and foot to my grandparents' house. When I arrived I pushed the doorbell. Chimes rang out but nobody responded to them. I walked round the back and pushed open the door.

The kitchen was sparsely furnished. The table was still against the wall. The windows still opened to the garden. But the kitchen was lighter, more modern. The plush leather car-chair which one of my uncles had put on heavy wooden rockers was gone. I searched my memory for other furniture but the best I could come up with was the presence, perhaps, of some thin chairs or long-legged brown stools. The dark hallway had opened up. Gules which the stained-glass door shone on the carpet were gone. Plain glass stood in the frames. A spiral staircase with none of the heavy varnished guardrails swung up to a large room with large windows. A carpet was on the floor but there was no furniture. Suddenly, I remembered seeing my grandmother downstairs. She had been against the wall near the table, silent. I looked around, and it occurred to me that the divider between the two duplex houses had been knocked down, and that was why the room was so large. Two houses had been made into one, at least upstairs. I went downstairs again.

My niece whom I hadn't seen since she was a baby came over and gave me a hug. Her other uncle was playing with a plastic spider which he flicked around the room on the end of a long string. The child was very loving and hung onto my neck.

"Where's your mother?" I asked.

"In the basement, washing," she replied.

"Let's go and see her," I suggested.

The basement was filled with open refrigerators. I chose an icecream on a stick and bit into it. The label said there was a filling, but no matter how deeply I bit I could find no trace of a filling. My sister was at the sink. Water was splashing like a fountain. I was appalled at the waste, and the phrase "Pollution of all our streams and rivers" leaped into my mind. The words stunned me. Streams as well as rivers. Streams, in the remote countryside. Then I remembered there was no remote countryside any more. The valley where I used to tend the cows on summer nights, sitting and sucking clover for the nectar or cutting open thistles for the nut; lying beside the cows at night, hearing their churning stomachs and breathing in their clover breaths . . . It had all been terraced for a housing development. Where I used to collect cabbage-white butterflies and go bird-nesting, houses were there too. There were no sacred places left anymore. The steam of clothes washing got into my nostrils. I threw the rest of the icecream away.

On the way out I passed my grandmother again. She sat staring straight ahead. In my mind's eye I saw shrunken heads and bodies such as those found in Danish peatbogs, strangled sacrifices to the Earth-goddess.

I ran into the town, and pulled up straight. All the wartime damage had been repaired, but instead of a modern town rising from the ashes, something like a medieval village had been constructed, meticulous in all details. The docks were paved and clean, and a large ship had docked behind the memorial steel lifeboat. Across the water an island seemed to rise.

TWENTY-FIRST

In my present (no doubt temporary) capacity as Assistant Health Inspector I thought I would be able to do some good, but my activities seem restricted to coming into contact with more weirdos than I thought existed. And a job like this can do funny things to a man.

I remember once I found myself investigating a complaint on the Lower East Side. I trudged up narrow stairs, opened the unlocked door, and walked in. There was no furniture in any of the four rooms, but the last room had a fridge. Two hippies, a young man and a younger girl, were crouched on the floor.

"Are you selling the fridge?" I asked.

The girl pulled herself up, glassy eyed, and opened the fridge to a heap of stinking food on the bottom.

"Sure," she replied. "And the other smaller one under the sink. And the Garbage Disposal Unit. And the toaster, the new one that does two slices at once."

"Someone already wants that, baby," droned the man.

She looked at me.

"What about paying for the silver watch?"

Silver watch? Slowly it came back to me. That was where I'd first met her. Was it why I'd come up there? I couldn't remember whether I'd paid her or not.

"Put it on the bill," I said.

I looked up. There was no roof. The overlapping tenements gave some shelter, however, but I was briefly blinded by what seemed to be the full moon, sun-bright, hitting a cloud right in the middle, and coming through.

"Doesn't it get cold in winter?" I asked.

"No," she replied.

"And when it rains?"

She looked up.

"We don't feel it."

Both of them looked up at the cloud-moon. Then the girl moved closer to me. I felt her hand on my thigh, and I was briefly aroused, but threw it off. I had a job to do. Something about child abuse. But there was no child.

Just then, I turned as a flash of light illuminated the darkest part of the room. A cage. A pair of large horny feet were pressed flat against the wire mesh. Suddenly I knew that, wrapped in filthy cloth, there was a baby there. One they all take turns in abusing sexually, if the sources of the complaint are correct. I was horrified. Just then, luckily, the doctor from the Board of Health who had been sent after me entered. I turned, and pointed out the cage. He went over and reached for a piece of newspaper on the floor. He bent over the cage and wrapped a piece of dung in the paper. He threw it on top of the wire cage.

"Do something," I said to him.

The doctor peered closer, looked inside, carefully, professionally. Then he started to take off his jacket.

"It's a cute baby," he murmured. "A very cute baby . . ."

TWENTY-SECOND

My life is not all fun. In fact, there's not much fun in it at all. So now and then I go to watch hockey, just to relax. I used to frequent one famous rink more than any other, initially for the soothing effect of its mindless violence, but then because of the captivating presence of the coach's daughter.

I remember one evening vividly, when we almost met. I had made a habit of buying a seat right behind the bench, for that was where she sat. I managed, on this particular home game, to side up to her. I sat waiting for her move. She shook out a cigarette from its pack and lit up, even though she was far too young to smoke, and there were No Smoking signs everywhere. She threw away the match, which landed on the skin of my arm and burned into it, like a brand into ice. I sat like the Spartan boy with the fox in his bosom. The pain was terrible, but much too painful to be taken out. And the game was well under way.

As the game progressed slowly I pressed the skin from both sides as if I was squeezing a pimple. The blackened match-head rose to the surface. I took it out. The wound mouths closed slowly. I felt very relaxed.

TWENTY-THIRD

Sylvia was more my type, though I fought against the fact since I needed all my attention to focus on the duties of my new job, that of probationary store detective.

One day I was in the store, talking to Sylvia. She wanted me to show her round, so, a little nervously, I agreed. We needed the elevator to get to the third floor (womans' clothes), but we had to go to the third floor to get it. From there the complications multiplied. It was one of those days.

A girl ran up and asked me if I'd gone to college with her father. She was blonde, so I imagined that her father must be blonde too, and look like her. But I said no, even though I knew she was asking for my help. Then, seeing that work would have been impossible that day, I snuck out with Sylvia, and we went to the ballpark. But I couldn't forget the girl, so, when the game had just gotten under way, I had the girl's father paged. (Sylvia, by the way, was not the baseball coach's daughter, though she was the god-daughter of Casey Stengel, or so she said).

They got out of the elevator which had taken us to our seats (good seats. As I said, Sylvia had pull). The father of the distraught girl got into the elevator as we were getting off. He looked just like her. That was how I knew. But he didn't stop to thank me. It was clear that he thought the whole episode very embarrassing, and was ashamed of his daughter for having panicked. I couldn't say I blamed him. Sylvia disagreed.

After the ballgame, Sylvia and I went to the beach. Lying on the hot sand, I told her all about myself. Then we went home in the car. I told her about myself, but she shut me up. So I told her about my former female teachers. Sylvia was driving.

"Look out!" I yelled, but we had already hit a young man who bounced off the hood of the car.

"It isn't serious," she said. But his buddies, a bunch of hoods, looked ugly. So I said to her, "Stay inside and close all the windows." But she didn't. Instead, being Sylvia, she got out of the car and tried to reason with the hoods, who grabbed her and started beating up on her. Then they reached into the car and grabbed me too, though the whole thing had had nothing to do with me. And all this, believe it or not, took place on Nassau Street in front of Nassau Hall on the Princeton campus. If you can't be safe there, where can you be safe?

Anyway, I slipped out of their grasp and ran to where I could hear some drums. As I ran, I could hear Sylvia calling out to the dancers for help. As I reached them and began to tell them what had happened, they laughed. They thought it was all a prank. I rushed back. One guy with a receding hairline and round face had Sylvia down on the ground. The bus for New York rolled by slowly, a few faces pressed against the glass, watching.

"Kick him in the balls!" I screamed, just as a fist found my mouth. Before I lost consciousness I saw the man step with all his bulk on her stomach and breasts, again, and again, and again.

TWENTY-FOURTH

I find woman God's best idea, and his first (at least, as far as the human race is concerned). Knowledge was her idea, and it was a physical thing, symbolized by an apple. Unfortunately, man came to believe that his head, roughly apple-shaped, was really the seat of knowledge. And hence all our problems. Take my case, for instance. I have done far too much reading. I always used to assume that what I read was true, had some kind of autonomous entity because it was visible and definitively phrased. Print has determined and ruined my life. I'll give you a for instance.

I once read a phrase and fell in love with it. The phrase was "soft brown doe-eyes." Soft brown doe-eyes rising at the outer edges like wings. Then I met a woman, and thought I'd met *her*, soft brown doe-eyes. I was ready to fall in love. But my reading had only focused on the eyes. It had said nothing about the mouth, so her mouth to me was a blur. I got out the book again and dug hard for a mouth phrase. But there was nothing that really struck me. I just couldn't come up with a satisfactory phrase. I have tried for some time, because I really like the girl, and now I discover that I dread finding it. For then I will have to find another for the ears, the hair, the skin, the brows, teeth, chin, tongue . . .

My God, is there no end to the making of books?

~

Women, then, have always fascinated and confused me. Take Tatti, for example. She came in parts. She bore her vagina with her, and wore her breasts. Her hips swung outward as if offered to the first who could catch them. Even her face was separable, and the parts of her face. Every time

I saw her I was amazed that she carried her vagina around with her, and the clitoris tucked into its folds. To have it with her the whole time seemed a wonderful thing. And I having to work for it the whole time. And even when I came to almost love her and everything fell in place and she became too large to divide; and even when her past with its experiences lived about her and influenced the way she felt, and the way her intellect and intelligence and sensitivity would change me and change her changing me, even then, when I saw her coming toward me, I would be struck when I least expected it by the idea of her carrying her vagina around with her, something of infinite delight and pleasure, something tucked away, something I could never take for granted, a bouquet, a gift, something that didn't open its meanings till it loomed larger than it was, but something that was always there, even when she was being most intellectual, even when she was asleep, even when it turned purely fictional, or functional and bled, or squeezed out a child. When I entered her, I tried to envision myself, watch myself, because otherwise I would have sworn that my whole body was being held tight, and not just that most ridiculous mouse, my penis. I could never equate copulation with my feelings. When we made love she was all vagina, all mouth, all tongue, all lips, all teeth. The legs with their heels pressing me in the small of the back led down along the smooth flanks into the vagina. The arms drew me in. I was awash in the great sea, the great thalassa. At a formal dinner, I could not equate her cool logic and decorum with her open body on the bed, and she would start to come apart again. The only way I could hold her together was to stifle my yearning for her. It made her more luscious, more ripe, *more*. My fingers and tongue sought her, more than my penis; for the vagina received and gave back scents, to and from the whole body. That body remembered from the days even before there was a body. Just a cell struck by lightning in primal ooze. That primal cell from which we are all descended, all descended.

TWENTY-FIFTH

One day I was walking Lotte to the bus.

"There's Peter!" she said, pointing.

"No," I replied patiently, "it's not Peter. It's very like Peter, but it's not Peter. It's his ghost. They're very much alike, but not identical."

(Peter, you must understand, had been a recent lover.)

"Oh," she murmured, obviously disappointed.

"Look," I said. "Don't go home yet. Let's go to a movie."

She brightened immediately.

"A movie! A movie!"

She almost ran all the way there, as if it was the first movie she had ever seen. In fact, I believe it *was* the first movie she'd ever seen, having been brought up in a very strict Lutheran household.

When we got to the theater the movie was well under way. A huge penis was in mid-orgasm. Lotte came to a dead stop in the aisle as there was a great welling up of sperm and then an overflowing of thick whiteness for what seemed eternity. She collapsed into the nearest seat which, luckily, was unoccupied. The penis continued overflowing. It must have been a time-lapse sequence.

"It's the first time I've ever seen anything like *this!*" she croaked.

"What! A time-lapse?"

"No. A penis!"

She was obviously upset. So I told her not to think of the scene as real, but as a kind of ghost-image, and that quieted her down somewhat. At any rate, when the movie ended she asked me to take her to a bookshop, which I did, thinking Peter might be there and I could get her off my hands and spend the rest of my vacation in the library.

When we arrived at the bookshop it was clear that things had changed. It had been converted into a hardware store. I'd worked there some years before, but the change didn't faze me one bit. I looked around for Catchpole, and found him hammering a nail atop a ladder. Calling up to him, I introduced the girl, whose name I had unaccountably forgotten.

"I've never seen *anyone* climb so high!" she gasped. Then she pointed out the window.

"That's P–," she was about to say when Catchpole yelled down a riddle to her.

"What stands up in bed, brings tears to your eyes when you grasp it, and is strong when you put it into your mouth?"

"An onion," she yelled up at him, preoccupied with what she thought she had seen. Catchpole, meanwhile, was so mortified that he fell off the ladder and lay at her feet, a crumpled unaesthetic object.

"You're home and dry now," I told her. "If you survive. Now you've got two ghosts to reckon with, and one of them is the ghost of a dead man."

"Oh dear," she whispered. "And we weren't even engaged."

I should imagine that by now you can guess the end of this story. Lotte and Catchpole's ghost got together, out of mutual sympathy, perhaps, or mutual admiration, or perhaps because there's nothing more confusing to a red-blooded young woman than having a 'lover' who's never 'loved' her, whom she can't find, and who has a ghost before he's dead. Catchpole was at least one up on Peter.

And so now she enjoys all the joys of carnality with a spirit, thus eternalizing, so to speak, that most evanescent of all joys, the moment of bliss itself, when the vital juices go out from the body in a kind of ghostly perpetuation, and mingle with the juices of the other, thereby creating a mediation or bridge between essence and flesh. Thus flesh was retained virgin for her, while forever (or at least for a very long time), realms became one and she, thus infused, is trans-substantiated to the point where, one day, she will look back and see her body walk away, seeking perhaps, in a misguided but understandable way, the body it once lost, solid in the land of the living with her Peter, and perhaps, if she is fortunate, as she looks she will begin to realize that it is precisely in that land of the living where real life can never be said to reside.

TWENTY-SIXTH

Lotte and I could not stay apart for long. We were *very* very fond of each other. So we decided to meet at the Lyceum for a matinee performance. It was a lovely performance. A lovely performance. As we were leaving we were attracted to a crowd listening to a busker singing in Spanish. Lotte, carried away, joined in, but a fat lady turned and snapped:

"He's singing in Spanish, but you're singing in German-Swiss."

"But I *am* German Swiss," replied Lotte, bristling.

After I took Lotte home, I went back to my own house, where Mrs. English, my cleaning-lady from Trinidad, was showing her 17 year-old daughter how to wash the pile of dishes I'd let pile up during the week. I had hardly taken off my shoes when, turning to me and drying her hands on her apron, Mrs. English asked me to devirginize her daughter. It had something to do with Trinidadian rites, I believe. But I wasn't paying attention since I was still relishing Lotte's reply. At any rate, Mrs. English, hands nice and dry, walked over, unzipped my fly, took out my penis, stroked it vigorously, and scrutinized its swollen red head. Then, beckoning her daughter over, she tossed her skirt over her head, made her turn round and bend over. Mrs. English thrust my penis into her daughter, whose vagina seemed endless. I went in and out, jerkily, my heart not really in it. Mrs. English snapped me out of my reverie.

"Do you have any habits?" she asked.

"No, only habits," I answered, not really paying attention, still relishing Lotte's reply.

Mrs. English's voice rose.

"Are they habit forming?"

"No," I said. "Only if excessively indulged."

Just then I made the mistake of opening my eyes and looking over the daughter's back. I saw there were no fingers on her right hand. I knew at that moment we'd never be happy together and could never fulfill each other's aspirations.

But it was still a beautiful day, and the house was spotless. It was a very narrow house. Through the window I could see Jinny, the rather stupid Irish setter, putting her paws on the edge of the rainbarrel. You could almost see the whole sky through the house because the front door wouldn't close; it opened outwards and the house tilted slightly toward the street. Lilac was in bloom, and I felt that, perhaps, falling in love wasn't entirely out of the question once I withdrew and requested Mrs. English to do likewise. There was a hedge of lilac across the street, tufts reaching upward. I exonerated Spring from any malign intent, because it had been and gone so often before with absolutely no results. No, the decision I made was strictly my own. I hate having people or things make up my mind for me.

But we were not happy. I knew things would not go well when a lord came up to us in the ball-park and I shot him dead with one bullet from my Saturday Night Special. I hadn't been feeling well all day, and my *malaise* was particularly acute at the ball-park. I blame the fact on a couple of things. One, although we had paid for covered seats in a semi-private box to watch the Yankees strive for their first pennant, we were in fact watching the Mets on a very small TV set. And two, my awful jealousy. Just the month before I had found in a shoe-closet her diaphragm, the one shaped like a rubber nest, with red jelly and sperm in the middle. She told me who he was, though claimed not to be in love with him. I believed her when thousands wouldn't.

The lord incident was merely an unfortunate accident. He had nothing whatsoever to do with anything (though I have always had a peculiar aversion to lords and have not, from that day to this, regretted my action). As you can see though, my desire for vengeance was not slaked by one accidental death. When we got home from the ball-game I took a deep drink from the flat paper on my desk under the skylight. It slaked and satisfied. She came in later with her mother, Mrs. English, as well as a few friends who all intended to slake their thirsts at my paper. I stood aside and motioned them forward. As they bent to gulp, though, I slipped in among them and tore the paper to shreds beneath their noses. Through the open door of the tilted house came a wind to aid my efforts. It riffled papers and shreds so that not so much as a mite of confetti moistened their cracked lips. They went thirsty. I am lord of my paper. They will stay thirsty, but I know secret hoards. They will leave me in peace, all of them, to relish Lotte's reply and whatever other replies might happen to take my fancy.

~

Even when she married Philip, Lotte and I stayed close. I used to spend much time with the new couple. I recall one evening when Philip and I were both kissing his wife. She was even more beautiful now that she had settled down in matrimonial bliss. After a while, Philip disengaged and left the room. I went to bed, as easily as if I had been in my own house in my own room. I slept, but in a half-doze realized that Lotte was in the bed beside me. Sweet girl! I reached over and ran my two middle fingers round her left hip—she had her back toward me. She gave off seventy-seven short metallic farts. I relished them! I relished them! What a woman! What a woman!

~

It should come as no great surprise after all I have said that women obsess me. I can't take them or leave them. Even when I leave them I take them. I'm surrounded by them, their scents, their sight, their whole mythology. I can do almost nothing without thinking of women, and most of what I do has women as a motive, even celibacy.

This fact should shock no one. Celibacy is the most sensual of denials. One possesses all the women one has ever known and at the same time denies them, at least in the kind of celibacy I am noted for, which is acquired and not inborn. In this kind of celibacy one can have the women forever. It is a totality, even if a totality of opposites. In actual possession there is no possession at all. There is the moment and the loss of the moment. The moment *itself* is lost. For ever and ever. Memory is no substitute. Celibacy, however, reinstates perspective. It prevents more loss. Working with time, it steps out of time. Its denial is due to excess of sensuality, not paucity. Building the self in a selfless zone, it is able to reinstate the full spectrum, and it only can see all the colors. Celibacy is the self's tree growing out of all that is not self. It is health.

Celibacy is a stage in human evolution, the last. Not, like homosexuality, a slipping into the physical dissolution of the race, but the last light step in a progress that began with the small Javan stoneknapper, Australopithecus, and the mute little African, Pithecanthropus. That first stumbling step freed their hands. The stretch upward took the brain with it into new air, into a new world, real and fantastic. Nature's vacuum was filled, like the cranium itself, with new sights which were stored in spiritual code, symbols so concise they outweigh the physical world, something like those black stars that are invisible because the weight upon their surface is so great not even light can escape. Man lived in the spirit, a spirit steeped in the actual. Celibacy continues the process of concentration. In order to be pure essence, at one time or another the celibate suffuses himself with the physical. As. . .

Out of the crowd I picked a woman in magenta, skirt to her calf, long legs, full hips, competent breasts. She walked as if history had never taken place. A bus nearly hit me as I turned to cross the road. I timed my entrance exactly. I cut across her wake about three feet after she'd made it. The scent was still drifting and the air disturbed. I didn't even turn to watch her. I had entered her wake, at right-angles. Then I recrossed the street. I could accept the impossible. I had made contact. I had crossed the street, and crossed back. I had improved it. I had improved myself. I had improved the woman.

When the race grows extinct in the near future, those males who practise celibacy (all of us by then), will not have been dragged down with it. *We* shall exist for ever. We shall be happy in our secret expanse, in our choice, despite the fact that many of us had been mistaken in our time for dirty old men, frustrated, celibate only for lack of opportunity and personal attractiveness. But a genuine celibate would never feel up a woman on the subway or squeeze a breast on a crowded bus. We would, however, look up a wind-blown skirt, for this is a sign of advanced civilization, this displacement of the urge, and not at all inconsistent with the true meaning of celibacy.

In *Civilization and its Discontents*, Freud said that upright posture reoriented us from smell to sight, and hence shifted the sexual stimulation of males from cyclic odors of estrus to the continual visibility of female genitalia. Now, a dirty old man would much rather see a glimpse of panties, for at heart he is only a fetishist. A celibate, however, as he looks up a skirt, always hopes for a glimpse of the genitals. A dirty old man lives in time. We aim at the mystery. We exist for the spirit, which can have no time scale. Our eyes are the home of the soul.

When a spaceman from another planet arrives, we will have done our job. Fundamentally, all males wish to escape into essence. Even the sight of menstrual blood scares them because it reminds them of mortality, aging, and death. Each man believes in eternal youth. Gradually, all men will choose our way. Women will try so hard to liberate themselves from biology and history that they will isolate themselves. There will be no reason for men and women to come together, and each will go their own way, free at last.

When that spaceman (or woman, probably woman) comes to dig in the former USA (or Europe, or any other industrialized country) he or she will expose only the skeletons of women, white, buried in a standing position. He or she will naturally assume that this was a race of females. There will be no remains of the males, for we will have turned to air. How can the spirit have remains? We shall have evolved into whatever thin air there is left. We will become an indistinct as water is in water. We shall have become the highest point on the evolutionary ladder. Air.

TWENTY-SEVENTH

A short time ago a funny thing happened. Well, not funny exactly. All week I'd taken care of my cat whom I'd allowed to be castrated after three years of rough tomhood because the vet said his recurrent cystitis was caused in large part by "tension." Remove testicles and you remove tension, he'd said. I had had nightmares all week. The theory seemed to be working well, however, until one night when the cat blocked once more. He took himself off to deal with his pain alone in the big house where I lived, and I wasn't able to find him. If he remained lost for forty-eight hours he'd become uremic and die of internal poisoning.

Why did he do that to me? I'd fed him all his pills daily and nursed my scratches and bites silently. Been late for work as I chased him around and over the furniture. Got down on hands and knees to retrieve one red pill from where he'd chucked it up just as I was congratulating myself that it had gone down. I'd fed him chicken fillet which I couldn't afford for myself, "liberally sprinkled with salt," as the vet's parting sheet specified. I'd given him all the "love and affection vital for your kitty's full recovery." And he did *that* to me. I was afraid to go away for the weekend of rest I badly needed for fear of returning to a stiff moggy.

And it had to come to *this*. This . . .

All day I'd been driven crazy by lust, to the extent that I couldn't concentrate on locating the cat. I'd fought it down as long as I could until I could stand it no more. I still tried, however. I used cool meticulous planning to determine how I would obtain some pornography. There were three shops in the area that carried the stuff. I decided to walk to the farthest and then, if my nerve failed me, I could buy a *Post* or something and still have two chances left on the way home, hoping my courage would grow.

At the furthest shop a gang of children were buying comics, but there were not enough kids to grant me anonymity. My glances over the shelves couldn't pick out what I wanted, so I picked up the *Post* (a paper I never read) with an honest gesture, and was about to move to the cashier when the man next to me leaned down and took a *Playgirl* from the pile. I didn't want *Playgirl*—I'd been told more gays buy it than women—but I let my arm slide along the channel in the air his arm had opened and slid the magazine beneath the paper. I paid without looking at the cashier, and walked out. I had half-succeeded with half-courage. So I entered the middle shop, a place where I buy whatever paper I occasionally buy, so the man was slightly familiar with my face, and I with his. The shop was empty. I bent down and picked up a *Voice* with authority, and, swinging my arm to the left, found a *Screw* between my fingers. I was half tempted to slip the thing under my coat, but instead said the weather was fine though they predicted rain. I looked him in the eyes and held both papers out. He agreed it might rain and counted out the change. I didn't need the third shop.

But all this just made matters worse. Flipping over the pages at home, my guts still ached with lust, ached even at the pitiful thing sex becomes in the slick mag and the gritty rag. My guilt was mounting each minute the cat remained lost. I tried reading German poetry. I played Mahler. I played Johnny Cash. I called five women but they were out. I called another but she'd just gotten married. I called another, was overjoyed that she was in, and invited her to a threesome with a hypothetical third. I watched the Vikings and the Browns. I even went to the foot of the stairs and sang my cat's favorite songs. The house, emptied of all its tenants, echoed them. My stomach began to feel as if it hadn't been fed in three months. It began to drizzle. My legs began to ache. In the rain I walked to the gym. I left when someone complained to the proprietor that my sweat stank like a goat, and the proprietor tactfully suggested that I wear deodorant when I work out. Back home I read the porno movie round-up and the ratings on the peter-meter. I chose one that was 100%, and close by.

It was rather sensitive, as such things go, and shot in large part across the street from where I lived. I began to feel more comfortable as I picked out what I knew. The best scene was a threesome, and I could see my house through a window. Maybe the cat was in the attic! A short skit on a Bergman movie was also shown, so my mood was almost high when I left. But it was very dark. Rain splattered. My testicles cramped as my mood began to change to old despair. I was so fierce so suddenly my cock shrank into my groin. In my black overcoat with half its buttons missing I strode along, avoiding looking at the women. I was angry. I was *livid.* I was so angry I walked where gouts of rainwater fell from holey gutters overhead and soaked me till the whole of my neck was awash. I was hungry.

I passed the local deli that stays open until 2 a.m. all year round. Over the years, here I'd picked up those foods I denied myself at the supermarket because I put on weight easily and rapidly. I didn't go in often, but when I did I'd trick myself by waiting until the supermarket was just about to close, and then, deciding I needed essentials like milk and bread, I'd walk on up to the deli. There, in a rush, I'd buy cupcakes, candies, fig newtons, and take them home for a late night snack. On those nights I never slept a wink, and next morning my stomach was a morass, an acid fastness, and my conscience was bad.

I walked in and said, "Good evening, Dom." I walked to the back where the milk case sat under the convex spy-mirror. I saw some Port Salut, sliced and wrapped. Took it, and stuffed it into my pocket with its one glove (the other was lost over a year ago). Took a loaf from the other shelf. Came face to face with Dom.

"Can I help you, sir?" he asked.

He followed me and my "no thanks, I'm just getting stuff for the weekend," with

"Excuse me, sir, but do you have some cheese in your pocket?"

Me, with my dirty old black coat and its missing buttons and missing glove? Me with the pain in the gut? *Me?*

"Yes," I said. "But it's all going to be paid for. I just put it there. Easier to carry."

At the desk I met his eyes as we exchanged goods for paper money. Cracked wheat loaf, Port Salut, somewhat rumpled, No-Cal Black Cherry, no milk.

"And a bagel."

"What?"

"A bagel. Under that glass bell. No. Make that *ten* bagels."

"Three fifty."

"Here's four."

And I rolled out a wad and made sure he saw all the bills. We had a secret the line didn't know. He had helped me out.

"Good evening," I said, smiling. "And thanks."

He said nothing.

The brown bag began to get wet. I tried to tuck it under my arm. That damn cat. He could be dead by now. Gradually I realized I wasn't angry. I didn't know what I was going to do with the bag of stuff. And I'd forgotten catfood. But I had no cat, so what the hell. At the door I fumbled in the bottom of my pocket with its one glove, hugging the bag to me. No key. Must be in the other coat. No. There. The keys were wedged in the very corner of the darkest dark, stuck in a hole that was about to open and drop my keys where I'd never find them. I closed the door with a bang. Damn cat. Stinking damn cat. Gave half my guests allergies and sprayed on the other half. Well, he'd spray no more, poor little devil. Must be hungry. Getting lost makes you hungry. How the hell could he get lost in his own house? Out a window, maybe? But he always came back. And he wasn't lost, for chrissake. He was hiding. Tore up my apartment, shredded my pillows, slept in my best chairs till the seats caved in with his weight, threw up on the imitation Turkish rug, scratched my sofa to shreds. He must be in pain somewhere in the dark.

I sat down on the sofa. And immediately sprang up. He came out from under the Indian print, a little ruffled, yawning. I should have known. But he couldn't have been there the whole time. He stretched, gave me a whinny of recognition, and pretended he'd been there the whole time.

I found some frozen liver behind an ice-mountain at the back of the freezer, sauteed it. He sniffed the air and walked away. I crushed a red pill into it, for luck. He returned, rubbed against my legs, stretched his front legs and his chest like a stone heraldic lion guarding the entrance of an imperial palace. Settling to his task, he lapped delicately at the sides of his dish where the food was coolest.

~

When I settled down to read later, the cat jumped onto my desk and lay down under the swan-neck lamp. He purred while I read. I wondered why I loved him so much. I lay my bearded chin on his cameo pelt and asked him a question. A question I'd been thinking about for some time.

"Are you Jim?" I asked. "Are you my dear old dead grandad? Give me a sign."

He fixed his amber eyes on his tail and did nothing for a while. Then he bent double and took his tail in his teeth.

It came as no surprise.

~

Talking of cats reminds me of Janice.

When I made love to her I felt I was enjoying incest. I actually felt smaller than her, though that was far from the fact. I felt perched on her body, somewhat at her mercy. It was ridiculous.

She spent much of her time telling me about her love-life. She told me she once made it with Howard, her boss. He was her dream-doctor—"the white coat with the blood-spots, you know, turned me on." It was during Emergency. The bell had rung but Howard told them via intercom that he was already on an emergency.

Howard ran an Animal Hospital. Hence talking of cats reminded me of Janice.

She would tell me of women who seduced her in Guatemala in taxis, or how she and her friends used to masturbate behind their IBM typewriters in the advertising agency office where they used to work. And much else I've forgotten. She wore a cheap fur coat the winter that I knew her, and I joked about its origins, which upset her. As we walked, every time we rubbed against each other the hair came off in mangy clumps and stuck to my coat. When she bought a new suede coat the orange dye kept coating everything it came into contact with, including me.

One morning she stayed late because Howard had just become a decoy in Caesar's Palace massage parlor, checking on the girls to make sure they weren't hustling. He got free turns for his pains. He'd been getting into work late, and rather tired. Suddenly she jumped out of bed because she remembered that a woman client was arriving early with her poodle. That evening she returned and told me that she'd arrived too late. The woman had left a note, very angry.

"She works with retarded kids," said Janice. "The 'nice' ones with the social conscience are always the nastiest. And because Howard balled her once she is even nastier. Howard apologized to the bitch and took $20 off the bill. But I doubt she'll be back. When he balls them, I don't know what he does, but we never see them again. We just can't afford his sex habits."

It was almost impossible to have a serious conversation. New York was full of wonder for her. Sometimes it was a story about her gay friend Joe who had shown her a photo of a man with a twelve inch dick "who needed so much blood to fill it up that every time he got an erection he fainted." Other times she herself provided the wonder, like the day I went to the vet's to pick up some pills for my cat. Suddenly, from the luncheonette across the street, I heard "Look! No bra!" My head jerked up and there, flying towards me through the traffic, was Janice.

"No bra!" she called. "Don't they look nice under this sweater?"

Before I could answer, she had the sweater lifted up to her neck, flashing in the middle of the avenue, with the temperature around freezing.

"Come on into the office," she said, giving the finger to "those rude drivers."

We approached the door. "Let's ball on the operating table," she whispered. But someone was waiting for her when we got inside. An astonishing woman was sitting beside a dog. She was, apparently, one of the porn queens Janice had told me about who lived in the area, and whom Howard had, for want of a better word, befriended. She was dressed in little girl pink and had pink bows in her hair. Likewise her miniature poodle. Janice became businesslike, motioning me to a chair.

"Name please!" she almost barked.

"Anytime."

Janice looked up.

"Name please!"

"Anytime."

"Anytime? What do you mean 'anytime'?"

"That's my name. Anytime. Annie Anytime. I like it anytime."

"What appears to be the matter with your dog?"

Annie Anytime tucked the animal under its tail.

"Anal glands," she said.

"Oh, those!" said Janice in disgust. "I ask Dr. Levine to aim the dogs the other way when he squeezes them. I sit in my office with the door open and often he only just misses me. Once a doctor got it all in his hair and all over the walls."

~

That Thanksgiving, Janice had to go and see her divorced mother who had married a dentist in Miami—"a dirty old bastard. A pillar of the synagogue who stuck his hand up my skirt the first time we were introduced. I yelled at him and threatened to tell my mother. I got him up to two free fillings before I promised not to tell." When she was away I went to a party that consisted of five young gays, a middle-aged woman in black, who name-dropped all evening, and the hostess with her daughter. I realized slowly that I'd been invited for the daughter. Just before dinner, I went into the kitchen to escape the boredom of the living-room. "Not a very nice reason," said the mother when I told her the reason for the exodus. So, non grata, I left for the goose that had been deposited on the table. Dry. Everything else was candied: candied kumquats, candied crab-apple, candied peel, candied this and candied that. The main course was mainly stuffing. The woman in black sat beside me and kept asking "Do you know the French crowd in the art world? Jean X and Michel Y and Antoine Z," and so on. I said "I'm not in the art world."

"But you're French!"

"Am I?"

But she never gave up with her hows and whys and whens. Eventually she got the message and turned to one of the gays who was designing some stairs in Utah.

"Oh," she shrieked, "stairs! Oh, it's *epic!* I love epic things!"

I couldn't wait for Janice to get back. Unfortunately, she'd had to stay a few extra days. During that time, my cat got sick again. Howard had closed for a ski-trip, so I went to a place I'd seen advertised which specialized in cats only. The door was opened by a woman who looked as if she'd worked Las Vegas. I explained the trouble.

"You look like a show girl," I remarked.

"I was a Playboy bunny for five years," she replied.

"So I'm used to working with animals."

"I – "

"What's your sign?"

"My sign?"

"Your astrological sign."

I pulled a face.

"No idea."

"Well, you must know your cat's sign."

"Afraid I don't."

She was sorrowing, but patient.

"You must know when he was born."

"I don't understand how that affects anything."

"Well it does!"

Promising to do my best to find out the animal's sign, I withdrew. She should have been able to guess my cat's sign just from looking at him. The same went for my sign. Everybody remarked on how alike we looked. I began to distrust her, and decided to leave with my cat, and wait till Howard returned.

Unfortunately, when Janice got back her cat Gerald had died. She was full of guilt because she hadn't liked the cat from the first. Just before she left she'd said: "Gerald, I hate you, Gerald." He died of a blood disease, and couldn't breathe. She unravelled the sad story for me. Apparently, she'd taken Gerald in after Howard had had him shipped from California, imagining that, since he was a Himalayan, he'd be a status symbol and do strange things to attract the ladies, like walking on the end of a lead. But when the cat arrived, Howard, instead of being instantly gratified, was instantly disappointed, took a great dislike to him, and wanted to ship him back. He told Janice, when she protested, to have the cat put to sleep. She told him that she couldn't play God and took Gerald into her own apartment in Queens. He was sick, and she had to borrow money for his unsuccessful treatment.

She was still crying the day after she got back.

"Pull your tits together, girl," she exhorted herself. To get her mind off the cat I asked her about her step-father, whom Gerald had knocked from her mind.

"He was *disgusting*" she said, wiping her eyes. "I've a good mind to tell my mother, though she probably knows already."

"So what happened?"

"Oh, nothing much. He just tried to persuade me to wear my mother's high heels and step on his testicles saying: 'That's as close as you're ever going to get to *my* pussy'!"

"Come," I said, "I'll walk you back to your office."

As we arrived, Janice looked through the front window. She drew back.

"Oh, no," she muttered. "It's that old fool again. Last time he came in he had a dog on the end of a rusty chain. It had been there for 12 years—they had lived that long together and the man was too scared of the beast to take it off. Howard had to drug the dog before he could get close enough to take the chain off and examine it. There was nothing wrong. Healthy as rain. Let's go round the back way."

There were stacks of cages with animals inside. I stopped in front of one which contained a tough, large cat.

"What's that?"

"That? That's Crunch."

"What a funny name."

"He does what his name says he does. We can't get near him. We phoned the owner to come and hold the beast, but he couldn't understand how it was being so difficult."

"Did you give it its name?"

"No. The owner did. That's why we couldn't understand how he couldn't understand that we were having trouble with his little pet."

Soon after this, Janice and I sort of drifted apart, what with one thing and another. But I gave her a call after Christmas. I asked how she'd been.

"Not how. Where," she replied. "Been to the g.y.n.," she spelled out. "He said, 'Janice, I don't know what you look like. All I ever see of you is down here'!" She laughed.

"I thought I had VD last week. I decided to try another doctor, just for variety, and a friend gave me the phone number of one she used. I went in and he told me to strip. I did. He felt my groin. 'Nodes,' he said. I asked him what they were and what was the cause. 'Your feet,' he said. I burst out laughing and he lost his temper. He said, 'Put on your clothes. I like you better that way anyhow.' And all the while he'd been holding his knee against my crotch, like they all do. And few of them have nurses present. Then he starts asking me questions like: 'How often do you have sex?' —as if anybody counts. And 'Does your boyfriend do you in the ass?' And I start stuttering 'Er, well, sometimes, well, hardly ever.' And he starts telling me I'm too young and I start defending myself—I never even had to defend myself to my own mother! And I say something stupid like, well, er, we were engaged once. For a week. And then I got hysterical and rushed out. I asked my friend if the doctor was always like that and she said he was, but she was used to it. His daughter went to Europe last year and got the worst clap anyone had ever seen. Then she got pregnant and tried to abort herself by throwing herself down a flight of stairs. Then she got trichinoma. She worked in a shop and kept bumping against the cash register. She was going crazy."

And that was the last time I talked to Janice, though once, some months later, someone called and hung up. I don't know what it was about the silence, but I was sure Janice was at the other end. I called a girl friend of hers some days afterwards, and asked about Janice, but the girl hadn't seen her in some time. There was a rumor going round though, she said, that Janice was working in a massage parlor on 8th Avenue. She'd called her a couple of times but there was no reply. I myself called, but got no answer. At the office they just said she'd left.

Then, a few months back, I was going into a all-male hot action movie and thought I saw her outside, but she disappeared before I could see if it was her. In the movie I spent the time watching a man who lit a cigarette. The glow bounced up and down in the dark.

When I got out the woman was by the car-lot, snow piled all round. I pushed through the filthy snow. But it wasn't her. Her face was hard. It had none of Janice's mysterious gentle vulgarity. Her hot pants couldn't have kept her very warm. I said to myself: It's not Janice, but I'll take a turn round the block, and if she's still there when I get back I'll go over. But she wasn't. Another girl was. Sweet, toffee-featured face. I said hi. She said hi. I said to myself: If she's there when I get back from walking round the block I'll go over. I walked, saying to myself: Hi, honey. Pretty cold, eh? It's colder in Boston. What are your terms for making an old man warm? But by the time I got back she was gone. Each time I rounded the block a new girl was there, each one less attractive than the one before, thinner and more concave. After who knows how many turns round how many blocks I got back, and there was nobody there. If there's nobody there when I get back, I said, then I'll go home. When I returned there was a gay cruiser being a caryatid for the corner of the parking-lot kiosk. Just then, a car pulled up and hot pants stepped out. If she's still there when I get back, I said, I'll strike while the iron's still hot. The black snow stretched all round. The frozen slush came in again over my boottops. I got so I couldn't feel. Maybe it wasn't hotpants I wanted, nor even Janice, nor the nice girl who said hi. Or maybe it was. I would have liked one of the girls to have taken me home. I would have said: Just relax. This one is on me. Can I make you some cocoa? Coffee? You don't have any? OK. No big deal. It's nice here . . . But in my reverie, on the corner of 2nd and 14th I slid into the big woman who had been pregnant in the summer but was off the streets for only three days. "Punk!" she hissed. I would have liked to have told her she reminded me of my aunt, the barmaid, but I didn't. I opened my apartment door and snapped on TV. There was a man in a mouse costume. He was doing a shuffle, a kick, pfaa! He spread his arms out wide for applause. He didn't get any.

I went to bed.

his penis is in her mouth. the soot is falling down the chimney. a rat is dying in the corner of the garden behind some lumber. electricity is jumping the filaments in the bulb. the trucks are rolling down the street. weeds are coming through the thin soil of dust. the soot falling. the rat dying.

TWENTY-EIGHTH

I am not proud of being a pervert. Having a strong imagination, however, at once adds fuel to my perversity and excuses it as merely an exercise in innocent invention.

I have always loved trees. I have always loved being around or in trees. They have a maternal presence.

I was on vacation. I'd seen it the first day I arrived: a white pine, tall, clean-limbed with thick tufts of blue-green needles. I decided to climb this tree before I left.

The hot August sun dried the dew from the grass. I left the rented cottage and followed the deer path. The flicking of the pages of the *New York Times* she was reading grew fainter and fainter. The brush was thick, but I soon picked out my pine. The needles had made a brown carpet underneath, where nothing grew; a covered clearing. I bent down to get under the low skirt of branches, and close to the trunk where I saw the droppings of some animal, gleaming still, blackberries and seeds in the dark purple. There were also rabbit pellets and some deer fermets—the medieval word I liked though I hated the hunters whose name it was. I picked up a pebble of grey-veined quartz, sperm-grey, near the trunk. I broke off some small dead twigs to make my ascent easier, and accidentally tore off a twig that was still alive. I brought the broken end to my nose and breathed the scent. Then I rubbed it between and over my fingers. Resin. My favorite perfume. Amber, my favorite jewel. I reached above my head to a large branch and swung myself up till my feet could stand on two branches a couple of feet apart. I straightened up and looked around. The other side of the valley was blue. I looked at my hands, expecting to find some dirt or grime, but the bark was absolutely clean and so were my hands. A cicada scraped, and then a cricket. I looked around for insects' depredations. None. And no insects. I could see over the lower trees on the slope, but not the larger, so I looked about to see what I could grasp. I located two largish branches in a v from the trunk. I heaved myself higher and was presently taller than most of the trees around me. This was a great white pine, one of few left. In former centuries, agents for the King's Navy would have marked it out a mainmast. To my left, in a sycamore, the nest of a tent-caterpillar hung, brown crinkled leaves trapped inside.

Whenever my father went into the country among trees he would have to move his bowels. To that end, he always took a roll of toilet paper with him in the glove compartment, and a small shovel in the trunk. Thinking of this, my bladder moved. I turned to the sun-side of the tree and took out my penis. I directed urine into the light where its arc lit up and plunged in gold onto the needles below. Silently, a breeze got up. All the branches quivered. Those I was standing on, astraddle, went up and down like small ships in a swell. The needles shook off brightness like foil. A bird sang a few notes over my head. Then silence, except for the wind in the trees. I closed my eyes, and almost fell asleep standing up. Then I felt my flesh stir beneath my fingers. I looked all round. The Berkshires rose and fell; not a person in sight, not a human sound.

At first, I imagined the tree full of men, their organs hard and long, slowly stroking, and below a crowd of women, some naked, some in loose Greek gowns, loose and airy. Somewhere among the trees a flute, Pan-pipes, Lydian airs. Then my mind presented me with a tree full of naked women, legs open as they stood with a foot on two branches. The men below were looking up . . . But there was more excitement with the women below looking up at me, so I returned to that. And then I simply dismissed them all, and saw myself up a beautiful white pine, penis in hand, slowly moving the foreskin up and down, not intending to come, just letting the wind blow around my testicles; me, standing in a tall tree, looking over the entire countryside, and no one knowing I was there or what I was doing. My penis got stiffer as I heard a girl's voice from far down the valley, exercising a horse. I imagined unknown ample breasts. I loosened my jeans and dropped them. Then my underpants. The breeze riffled my pubic hair. My cock stood straight up and out, naked where I'd shaved it at the root. I cupped my balls in my left hand, the right stroking the shaft and then the glans. I concentrated on the glans with three fingers, and pitied the circumcised whose glans was not protected by the resilient foreskin.

The only fly I had seen all day came and landed on my hand, riding there as on a slow sea. Then it took off. I gradually became aware that the two branches I was standing on were shaking in rhythm to my strokes. I increased to a fast rhythm that threw light off the needles like water. The breeze set up a heavier rhythm in the surrounding branches, and played a counterpoint. I hadn't made love for two days. I could feel the sperm building up at the root, waiting to escape like magma. I grabbed my shaft and pulled fast. Sperm jumped out and landed along the branch a good six feet away. Some hung heavy from the tip of my cock. I caught it with my finger, and squeezed for more. I laid this thick fingerful carefully on the branch. The sun hit it. It seemed like the quartz pebble with its white veins in my pocket. The sun brought out thicker veins of white inside the hardening translucent caul. It began to look like cloudy thick woodsmoke inside a delicate membrane, delicate but tough. The tiniest fly I had ever seen landed on the sperm. It walked over it, turning upside down in the crags and crannies, trotting along the plains. I thought it might eat some, and hoped it would. But after exploration, the miniature flyer launched himself off into the wind.

TWENTY-NINTH

I often work and rework a memory until it has a title. This one is called "The Electric Blue Woman."

She was sitting on a chair, her long black hair falling over her shoulders. I stood in front of her. With her blue sharp eyes she was staring me into a statue. It was very exciting and very painful. While her eyes held mine in a grip of stone she had my penis at her disposal. I dared not look down, though I was hard and long and lay by the side of her wrist. With her thumb she jabbed now and then into my pubic bone, grinding her thumb into it so hard hairs came away. Sometimes, she ground her thumb into a testicle. At such times she would ask me questions like, There, isn't that nice? Or, Isn't this how you've always wanted it between us? Then she would grasp the shaft of my penis, still refusing to let me look down, and squeeze it as if she were ringing the neck of a chicken. I felt it would burst, but was almost unconscious. She refused to let my eyes cloud over. Her other hand reached behind and pulled down my shorts. She stuck her finger, the middle one, up my fundament as far as she could, fast, so it took my breath away. Her nails cut the delicate tissue inside the rectum, and I felt it almost up to my heart. She pressed hard on the prostate so I almost ejaculated, but she would not allow me that relief, and lessened the pressure. I was struck dumb. I had nothing to say. I wondered why I was standing.

Another woman, fully clothed, in the same outfit as The Electric Blue Woman, had a tight grip on me from behind. She had reached round to take my penis, her hand gentler, warmer. While The Electric Blue Woman jabbed me now and again in the pubis, the other woman would stroke my member and then, with a few flicks of her wrist, milk me of all my semen. "More, more!" they both commanded, and started the whole operation again. I felt like a fly being drained by a spider, a spider who had injected her dissolving spit into all the internal organs and then drawn in her cheeks and sucked hard. I wanted to yell "Rape!" but there were only white blank walls around me. I wanted the women to rape each other, but when I concentrated on this thought to ease the pain, my penis hardened worse than before, and the whole process began all over again. I was laughing and crying. "More," they hissed. "Hold nothing back. Hold nothing back. We'll come back for more. Make some more fast. We want it all. More. More!"

"You can have it," I moaned. "I don't need it. I'm giving you all I can."

But they just grunted, "More, more."

Tempting fate, I said:

" 'Menstrual blood is uncooked semen'—Galen."

For that the Women walked back, slowly, all in blue, flashing.

"Now there is no knowing what we are going to do to you."

THIRTIETH

They were walking their cats on leashes. I complimented each lady on her pussy. One was a lovely tortoiseshell.

"Only females are tortoiseshell," I said. "Right?"

"Right," one lady replied. "Only this isn't a tortoiseshell. She's a cameo."

"I thought only males could be cameos," I replied.

"Did you?" she said.

On the subway a man played a mandolin. "One night of love."

At the party, a bald Frenchman demonstrated in a thick French accent how blacks had said "shit" in 1941. And then he did an imitation of Churchill's "We shall meet them" speech. And then he did it again. And again. His baldness became very offensive.

Mirò sat on a bedside table. I flipped through. Somewhere it said, "The white fish illuminated." I wanted a pencil and paper. I searched the bed where she'd lain in connubial bliss. I put my foot on the pillow. Gallimard books were strewn about. I wanted to have lain there, but not in connubial bliss. Her husband managed a portfolio of forty million. My portfolio briefcase had a pencil in it, but I didn't know where he'd put it. There were mirrors on the doors. There were many doors in each room. I found it difficult to concentrate, so I began memorizing lines I'd never composed. I thought I'd never composed lines dealing with white fish illuminating, so I began to learn lines I might have written. They went something like the end of a song . . . That first time I'd met her I hadn't seen her shining finger. I'd fed her from my plate because she'd arrived late and all the food had gone. We'd gone dancing together. And to be invited to this dinner with her husband . . . She whose father had been a famous actor and protége of Diagilev after Nijinsky took off. Well. I got home late, just as Judy was opening the door.

"Gee, you look great, babe," I hammed, "in that Bangkok lamé dress. What yer doin' tonite?"

"I've already done it," she said. "It's one a.m."

"Got it," I said. "You've been to your coming-out ball."

"That's what Snoopy hasn't," she replied.

"What?" I inquire, stroking the poodle who's trying to shove his nose up my ass.

"A coming-out ball."

It was true. Like Hitler in the song, Snoopy only had one.

"Goodnight," I say.

"And you," she replies.

I walk up the stairs to my apartment, fumbling for the key.

~

I've been putting keys in locks for as long as my adult life has lasted. One key one lock. The doors all begin to look the same. Inside is the same landscape. With such lack of variety, how can I learn enough to speak of and for myself? How can I speak with the variety of tongues necessary for speaking to and for others?

The next night I went out again. I had become a going-out addict. I drank, smoked a bit, sang, fumbled for my key at one o'clock in the morning again. I hadn't done anything exceptional or said anything intelligent all evening. In fact, I had made rather a fool of myself. I had just made friendly noises. Next night the same. Except that on the way home I thought that, perhaps, I wanted to sleep with a woman. I went back to the party and cornered a woman I'd been working on all night before I lost interest. She had reminded me, for a short initial moment, of— well, never mind who. Then I found someone I knew. I soon got to the point. "It'll have to be chez moi," I insisted. "My cat needs to be fed pills otherwise he'll die."

And she said:

"Why don't you stay at my place?"

A little bored already, I reiterate:

"Because of the cat."

"Then come back after feeding the pills," she suggested.

But I was in no mood to compromise.

"Can't. Have to keep a close watch on him in case of a relapse."

So she said she couldn't come over. And I said, Well then, another time maybe. And by this time we're at her apartment house. She takes out her key and puts it in the lock.

What I had said about my cat was a pack of lies.

I couldn't talk to or for her.

So who else could I speak for? Somewhere along the line I am only me, and what I say after I've said it leaves me cold.

Walking home I saw a young man calling across the cold wet street, "What? What?" to nobody, and yet still calling as if he had missed their original comments or replies. Then, dropping English, he continued in a made-up language which he seemed more at home and fluent in. He continued to reply to the hypothetical comments and answers. I seemed to be the only person paying him any attention, and he ignored me.

The language I am coming to speak more and more is a highly structured language with plenty of declensions and parsings. Ideally, everything should agree, though in what is becoming my dialect things are not so tight. This dialect can in theory be translated into any other dialect, though the speaker can speak for nobody else and often not even for himself.

The growing body of literature is elusive. The poetry is echoic rather than consisting of full sounds. Every verbal hue has the white of reverberation added to it, while every tone has lost its complement, and so insists on fusing with the tone or hue nearest or most convenient. The result is that distinctions are hard to make and the full aesthetic force is continually shifting. Unfortunately, there is as yet no steady significant body of literary criticism to make the onlooker's job any easier. Still, it is possible to say some specific things about the language itself that makes up the literature.

All nouns derive from a root word meaning "key", and are parsed. The verbs derive from a word meaning "to open a lock," and are declined—many have declined themselves out of existence and there are only a few verbs left. Moreover, the original distinction between to open a lock and to lock a lock has virtually been lost.

As for the phonology, the language has suffered a series of sound-shifts demonstrating the reverse of Grimm's famous First Law, for the sounds have all retreated to the back of the mouth to become, for the most part, voiceless gutterals. Here, in addition, they run the great risk of banging into one another and becoming not only voiceless but confused and bruised. They are offered a certain protection, however, by virtue of the fact that there are so few sounds and words left in daily use. Still, it is undeniable that those vowels still in existence are remarkably monotonous, and the same can be said of the consonants, which express muffled throaty variations on the basic 'm' sound.

There are other shifts. Gradually, with the years, the furniture of nouns is being moved out at a faster rate than other parts of speech. The adjectival drapes are hung over those that remain, so that what is underneath becomes a matter more of interpretation and guesswork than fact or belief—often the drapes act deceptively and, upon close inspection, it will be found that there is nothing under the drape, just a kind of nostalgic vestige, a sort of shapely hankering. Eventually, it is to be expected that the adjectives too will drop to dust. As was noted earlier, the verbs are having a hard time too, perhaps harder than is realized by the speaker (me) who has no one to listen to and has adopted the habit of never listening to himself.

His key never falters, even if he tries to make it falter. The neighbors interpret his expert act of opening the door as a sign that everything is hunky-dory. They do not know that at the other side of the door is a country which might frighten them: a country which he had great difficulty in recognizing every time he entered. Eventually it has become a foreign land far removed from the original topography. He has almost forgotten the original topographical terms and place-names because each time he returns, the land has changed on his lips. For a while he tried using archaic words and phrases, and for a while the cat understood him. Then the cat changed and hissed every time he opened his mouth.

He is now experimenting with a language of total arbitrariness, and is having some success in quieting the beast's antagonism by a series of quasi-animal noises. Once or twice the cat has actually recognized him. Once or twice he has almost recognized the landscape his arbitrary key had fumbled open.

THIRTY-FIRST

I decided to leave my job and travel. Movement was in my blood.

First I went to Africa, on a ten-day excursion. Things went so fast I don't know how I got to the savanna, but get there I did. I sort of came to myself in a tramped-down area of grass with tall grass all round. I heard a crashing not far off and beat my stick against the earth to frighten the animal away. After a safe time, I slowly parted the grass, and saw a lovely palomino grazing. He lifted his head, and I could see his expression change. He saw me and charged. I came all the way to Africa to get charged by a horse!

The beast chased me out of my refuge and down a rockface, stones rolling away from under my feet. The horse even started landslides to try and crush me. I caught a glimpse of some workmen on the side of the mountain, and yelled out to them—"It's mad! Help! Aiuto! Aiuto! È mazza! È mazza!"

They stop stopped what they were doing, and leaned on their picks to watch.

"Mazza?" they said. "Mazza? You sure? D'you mean 'pazza'?"

Trust me to pick people who understood neither English nor Italian.

THIRTY-SECOND

On the way home, though I'm not Jewish, I stopped off in Jerusalem. I'm not Christian or Moslem either. But I always wanted to see Jerusalem. I think it had something to do with a Biblical epic my grandparents took me to see where Moses looked just like Charlton Heston.

My most vivid memory is of an Arab standing at the Wailing Wall. He had just descended from his camel. He rummaged in his saddle bag and took out a hammer and chisel. He gouged off one name in the wall and gouged in another, weeping all the time. He held his capuchin monkey steady on his back now and then, but most of the time the animal winced at each hammer stroke and screamed silently. The Arab continued, unmoved. I was very upset and began to weep too.

When I could stand it no longer, I too took a chisel to the wall.

THIRTY-THIRD

After Jerusalem, I decided to visit the other cradle of Western thought, but not for any philosophical reasons. My grandfather had told me I had to go and look up his relatives in Greece. I thought I owed him that much.

I had hardly arrived in the country, however, before the airport was closed and I was caught in some dragnet put out by the military dictatorship. My grandfather had told me in great detail, ever since I was a child, how to get to the village where his mother was born, so I easily eluded the interrogation of the soldiers and, with my adequate Greek, hitched and walked to the Mani. I passed for a city Greek though my reddish hair caused some wonder. But I told everyone to read their Odyssey. Odysseus had red hair.

When I arrived, people were being bussed out to escape the Fascists. People had to present their I.D. cards to the driver before being allowed on the bus. One man caught my eye. He was searching in his pockets, and was almost in a panic. But he found what he was looking for and showed it to the driver. Then, suddenly, he decided he wouldn't leave. I got closer. From the beauty of his hands he looked like a relative. I approached him as he was going back to his house, and asked him some questions. I was right. He was the son of my grandfather's cousin's brother. He took me inside with him. He was very nervous.

There were two rooms upstairs, small and cluttered but cozy. There was a glass door between rooms. The rooms were sunny. His wife was in a bed in the far room, and he introduced me to her. She ignored me. He bent down and put his face close to her neck. She said, "The children have been evacuated." Then she accused him of actually liking the crisis, of wanting to stay behind to relive his partisan exploits. He stood up and looked out of the window. He drew me aside.

"Just a few days earlier, the Fascists dropped objects in the street that looked like small jujubes and nipples. People thought they might explode and called the police. My wife picked one up. She was fascinated. She was terrified. It exploded in her hands. She was showered with very good art posters. Immediately we saw through the strategy of the local Fascists. It would have been one up for them if the posters had been put up on the walls, or taken home to decorate our rooms. Unanimously, we decided to burn them, even though we liked them, and the reproductions were obviously very expensive. We all felt good about this decision."

The man turned from the window and looked at his wife. Her words seemed to return to his mind.

"How can you accuse me of that?" he said. "My children are taken from me. I've lost everything I had. You're not well."

He went over and took her hand.

Just then three women came in, brushing me aside.

"Who are you?" my relative asked. The woman pushed by him in her white coat.

"That's the venologist," she said.

He looked puzzled.

"What's that?"

"To do with bladders," she replied.

Both women went into the bedroom behind the glass door, closing it. We were anxious, and looked at each other. After a while our anxiety turned to suspicion. Then our attention was fixed. Some sort of struggle was going on in silhouette on the glass door.

We burst in, but too late. I felt a chill come over me. His wife lay dead on the bloodstained bed. Some long thin wire lay by her side. It had obviously been pushed into her. One of the women was on the phone.

"You're too late," she said. "We may wait years and years, but we never forget. We are everywhere. We will be around for ever."

My relative ran up and hit her on the back of her neck with a rabbit chop. She dropped dead. He ran back into the other room, but two Fascists stood facing him, one smallish, the other thickset. They had guns, but he tackled them and got a grip on a Beretta. I ran out the door but my escape was blocked. The thickset Fascist stood back and mocked us. He aimed the gun slowly at my relative's head, and slowly squeezed the trigger. But the gun locked. And locked again. The smaller Fascist laughed.

"Even if he fired it," he said in a surprisingly sweet voice, "all you'd get is enough art-posters to cover the world. Do you think we're fools?"

THIRTY-FOURTH

My life seems to be one long misunderstanding. I lurch from one crisis to another. I will tell you one more story against myself and then call it quits. I can only stand so much. I'm sure the same goes for you too.

I was once invited, in my capacity as music reporter on a Canadian newspaper, to the set of a recording studio. A boy-soprano was singing a song in praise of some Scotsman who'd been slandered and misunderstood (it could have been Bonnie Prince Charlie—but he was Polish). Anyway, it was a song all about the greatness of the Scots. I sat down, as I'd been instructed, at a table on which stood a beer-can and a glass beermug decorated with a yellow tartan. I was beginning to take notes, when someone came through the door facing the staircase in the basement studio and started to sing, somewhat mockingly. Trying to help, I said to him, "Why not go all the way up the staircase itself and sing? He'll hear you better." But everyone in the studio turned round and told us both to shut up. The boy-soprano scowled at us both in mid-note. I felt very uneasy, and was thinking of leaving, when a very imposing and beautiful woman came in and told me to stand up. I did as I was told, but when she started to frisk me I restrained her.

"I never carry money in a wallet," I said. "I always use a paperclip."

"That's good," she replied, "because a man can hide his penis in a wallet."

"What on earth do you mean?" I asked.

She looked at me like a cat.

"I suspect you of pederastic designs on the boy-soprano," she replied, cold. "And that could ruin his voice."

I was amazed, and told her so. But she was already on my lap, getting curled up. She caressed me. I couldn't resist caressing her, even though I realized it was all a ploy, a set up. She suggested that we should go to her place. Knowing I was letting myself in for a lot of trouble, I agreed.

Such is my life. Nothing gets resolved.

THIRTY-FIFTH

It was that time of year when you try to retain what you thought you had. The old year was sinking fast. I was in a Greek place near the Port Authority. I'd just downed a couple of drinks as the table emptied for a *hassapiko* As they played, the band cracked jokes.

"Bring on the fish from the sea," yelled Eli, knee-bending.

"I want tuna," yells someone.

"Good fish tune-up," says the bouzouki.

"You want good tune up? We got good tune up in Astoria."

The pun wasn't heard, so Eli repeated it twice more. He had danced all night. All dances are the same to him. He danced Romanian, Israeli, Greek, Macedonian, Spanish, Polish, they're all the same. He had the band trained and danced, danced, all technically correct and even spectacular. He yelled, he leaped, he grunted, he grinned, he whistled. He said *olé* and *opa* and *bravo*. He clicked his fingers, he slapped his feet. And I said to the chair beside me: If you're outside you're not inside and can only onlook and regret. Either you're inside or outside. If you're inside though you can't see being inside. If you're outside you have the knowledge but no part of the act.

"I'm drunk," the man mumbled on the floor of the Port Authority.

"We know," said the cops, "but you can't stay here." And they picked him up one under each arm and dragged him out into the cold where he could be drunk all he wanted, and freeze to death.

A lady with old Chinese features went before me down the subway steps. She came to a machine. She stood before it.

"You've got a filthy mouth," she told it. "I've heard that kind of filthy talk before."

When I looked carefully, it was a machine where you throw your garbage through the grill and water swirled beneath to swush it all away in a maelstrom. I turned to myself and said: Am I seeing all this? Will you call me tomorrow to tell me I saw and heard what I think I did? The lady thought I was addressing her.

"Give me your phone number, then," she demanded. And, in a daze, I gave it to her. She was still stuffing the bit of paper into her pocketbook as she got onto the train.

"All daughters have filthy mouths," she said loudly.

"And I haven't talked to her since, and that's years ago."

When I got out at 14th., the cold was intense.

"He used the whole bed as a desk," I overheard one woman tell another on Bank.

As soon as I got home, my cat and I, we went to bed. My right ball ached, and I had difficulty sleeping. The phone rang.

"You told me to call you and tell you you were seeing all that you said," the woman's voice said. She then began to tell me her life story.

"Just tell me the most striking parts," I pleaded.

She did. Until 2 in the morning, or thereabouts. I must have fallen asleep in the middle because the empty phone noise from the dangling phone woke me in the late morning.

I woke, and told myself: You have to carry a jar of sterile water to wash your hands in. Then I left the apartment.

I came across a pile of mattresses outside an itinerants' hotel, all wrapped and trussed, thrown out with Christmas trees and other jollities. I said: They're all tied up. They must be diseased. I tried to lift one, but it was too bulky. I said out loud: "They need to be sterilized."

My right ball had ached since before Christmas. The previous New Year's Day I had gone blind for a few hours in one eye. I was passing water more than usual, more colorful. Hernia, I said, was in *A Midsummer Night's Dream*.

"Do Not Load Above Top," said the rubble container on its little metal wheels beside a gutted building.

"I have a jar of sterile water," I replied.

~

After I got out of the hospital, I walked round the dismal town again. I saw a woman, and stopped. There was nothing about her. So then, what was it? Standing at an acting-studio door, and looking in. Dumpy. The face, the rouge, and the door. The close proximity of rouge and door, face and wood, wood and rouge, paint and paint. She was in her late forties, that turn of the tide, that time of the silent shriek, turn of the lock. I knew what her apartment looked like, and I had only glanced at her. I saw her getting up in the morning, as in a movie flashback. I didn't have to rehearse the details as if I didn't know them. I knew them. I saw her make up her face. When I sat down later and thought about it, I was back in myself, fleshing out details—sloppy old slippers, baggy limp dress, hair like a mop, in curlers maybe, stockings over the bathtub, or pantyhose, and maybe over the shower-rail. But I stopped this fictioneering in time. I knew all about her, and she had never even seen me. I wouldn't recognize her again if I saw her. Mine was a vivid knowledge; not a rape, but a kind of vacant possession. Yet for that moment, and after, it struck and stuck, and I was walking along, taken over. I was taken over. I was not myself. But why her? Why not someone easy on the eye, young, my type, interesting? If I'd been a writer I'd have written about it, making it what it was not. As it was, I still had to fight myself not to theorize and imagine. But there was, really, nothing. Just the moment, and the burden of the moment. I had to lift it from its purity and do something about it.

~

We'd been living together about two months. I was right about the stockings over the bathtub and shower-rail. But she never wore pantyhose. She said they stopped her from breathing.

I was lying on the bed dreaming of lying on the bed. I was an actor in the first real idyll of my life, which goes to show you never can tell. She was outside on a handworked rug, wedges of all colors, sunbathing in the late Spring sun and counting spiders. She said through the open door: "If you leave a wet towel by the bed you'll have spiders in the morning." I watched three large dead oakleaves that had blown in through the door. I was thinking: Somewhere I will find people who do everything entirely different. I got up and went to take a leak, jetting into the deepest part of the bowl. I had told her that I often aimed at flies, but they were very agile. I have never pissed on a spider. I wouldn't dream of it.

It was getting chillier. She came in and I zipped her into her yoga suit in front of the huge window with all its plants and colored bottles, high webs and framed trees. She stretched her body and breathed deep. She asked if she could teach me some. I said "I doubt there's any need," and went into the kitchen. I opened the icebox. Apples, carrots, cookies, sandwiches, cheese, all with one bite taken out, all marked with her little sharp half-moon. She said: "My children think all food looks like this." I looked out of the window and noticed that the feedbox was empty. I broke up crusts of stale bread left there all winter, and went out. Bird-dropped seeds sprouted beside hyacinths. My beard was growing gray in the window reflection. I called in: "Do you know the derivation of 'greyhound'?"

"No," she called back. "Fast. It means 'fast'." "It makes sense," she replied from the lotus position in front of the plants that were dying when I brought them up from the city a week before. Now even the shape of their leaves had changed.

"Window means 'wind's eye'," I remarked. "How do you like that?"

"I like it. I like going back to the life of origins."

But it is the nature of idylls to pass.

~

I sit drinking coffee now, that's what I do.

I sat drinking coffee. She sat drinking coffee. My throat rose to meet the scalding liquid. Her throat rose to meet the scalding liquid. A joint swallowing was heard.

"I'm probably going to be able to paint again in a while," she said.

I bit into an English muffin. The crunch, I knew, meant the end of crispness and the beginning of awful sog. I reached out my hand for the cup.

"Where's my cup?"

She looked down at five cups on the floor, though she didn't reach down. Her legs were tucked under her.

"That one. I would know your cup anywhere by now. I could crawl along the floor and sniff it out. There could be seventeen coffee cups and I'd know yours. Like a mother seal knows her baby from among thousands on a wet rock, I could–"

I'd had enough. I hated the sound of her swallowing. I got up. The idea that we two over the years had consumed lakes of coffee and other liquids, pissed ponds, eaten mountains and shit hills made my stomach ill. All at once, the acts of eating and drinking became obscene. I went into the garden and watched chickadees at the feeder. They'd stab their heads into a pile of seeds, shaking off onto the ground more seeds than they speared. They didn't seem to be eating. More like a game. An exercise. I began to wonder about the logic of waste. Presumably seeds are expendable, if there are billions more seeds. Throughout evolution, I thought, that is the lesson drummed into the tiny brain of those birds: there are billions of seeds. Don't bother about every seed. For every one you get you'll miss a million and knock hundreds to the ground. Seeds are expendable. Birds too, then, I reckoned. They too must be expendable, if, as is more than likely according to the actuary's chart, or the law of averages, there will be bad seasons when there will not be billions of seeds and starvation will result. Survival, then, is simply hit or miss. And if birds are expendable, birds I love so much, I continued, then best to get on with things as fast as possible. There simply isn't time for "putting up." If something disgusts, then one should simply and quickly remove the cause. So, eating should be attended with the same efficiency as defecation. To hell with amenities. If the requirements of civilized behavior are based on hit and miss, then best to get on with things.

From that time on I dined alone. My wife, of course, protested. But she understood nothing of my reasons, so I didn't try to bother to explain. She got on with her painting. I took my meals with me to the outhouse, where I'd sit on the seat and eat off my lap. The advantages of such an arrangement need no elaboration. And I could watch the birds without interruption. They seemed much more poignant.

~

I spent more and more time in the outhouse. I began to have great thought and great ambitions. I decided, after a great deal of thought, to become a philosopher. Indeed, I decided I *was* a philosopher, and all I needed to do was to start writing things down. The outhouse became my study. I took in a plank of wood to put on my knees and serve as a desk. I brought in pencils and paper. I began to write a book on the origins of Western thought. It began:

"Platonic forms, we are told, are numbers in mystical relation, or ratios of numbers. Pythagorianism is connected to the belief that numbers of Forms are the heavenly shape of things. Plato must have possessed the desire to press back to an impossible original essence, but settled for the creation of an absolute." Unfortunately, that's also how it ended. I saw no point in piling up proofs and arguments. I knew I was right, so why waste the time trying to convince others? So I decided to be a travel writer. You don't have to prove anything. You just go somewhere, to a place that, as often as not, is boring and irritating. But by writing about it you can cheer yourself up and make things look much better than they really were. Or you don't have to go anywhere. You can read up, and then write. I wrote one piece that was based on a dream—but who would know? It, too, began, and became a fragment:

"I am standing on the old France-Italy border near Col de Vence in the Basses-Alpes. Across from the old border-house which is now used for goats, I am standing on flat slabs of rock that look as if they have been laid, or fallen from some massive temple. The baous in the distance drop like stone fists onto the coastal plain and the Mediterranean. I know the awful crassness of this coast, but I also know rock-pools and rivulets for bathing at the feet of these precipices. The land up here is lunar—the gardener says flying saucers land here—and is swept or eaten bare to the white rock."

But there I quit. It changed nothing. And I wanted to change things. So I decided one morning, there in my outhouse, to become a literary person. I began in a modest way by writing obituaries. Here's one I wrote for Mozart. It didn't quite come out right, but I still have a soft spot for it:

Mozart shifted his position. A suitcase lay open under his feet. A bird twittered somewhere under its covered cage. Mozart adjusted a cravat which was sitting on his Adam's apple. He stuck a surprisingly small middle finger of the right hand into a white key in the middle of the piano. The note displeased him. There's no sense in going on, he said. But Wolfgang, murmured his wife, a lady of insistent charm and notable lack of tact, there's the children to feed. Children? said Wolfgang, ripping the cravat from his neck and hurling it from him onto the wreck that had once been a sofa. The cat looked up, draped. What children? Our children, the lady insisted. There's Carl Philip Emanuel, and Johann Christian, and . . . Madam, said Wolfgang, about to chase the cat to recover his item of dress, Madam, you poor silly woman, dear Constanze, they're not our children. Those are *Bach*'s children.

("Mozart's funeral was the poorest possible. His body was laid in a common grave assigned to paupers.")

Unfortunately, writing obituaries, even imaginative ones, was a dead end. So I decided to try a more exciting genre, the major genre of our time, in my opinion. Namely, the detective story. Here is my best effort to date:—

A woman had been murdered in his small apartment. He picked up the phone to call for help. The operator said: "How can I give you the number if you only give me the name?" So he gave her the number and she gave him the name. He called again and asked for the police, but for a long time he couldn't get through. When he did, the desk sergeant told him: "We have a priority system, that's why you couldn't get through. We stack up calls and give priority to crimes still in progress, in the hope of apprehending the actual perpetrators at the actual time of the alleged offense." He hung up.

The man's girlfriend walked in. He noticed a pimple on her cheek.

"I see you've had a facelift," he said.

She denied it.

"A woman's been murdered here," he told her.

"I don't see any body," she noted, after a quick look round. "Perhaps you did it and hid the body."

He denied it.

"The door's open," he pointed out. "You just walked in. Anybody could have walked in. A friend of mine was here just a while ago. He could have done it."

"I still see no body," she persisted.

He took her into the middle room, the bedroom.

"Look," he said, pointing. "A streak of blood. And a little pool."

She remained unconvinced. He got angry at her.

"You whore!" he yelled, and grabbed off the table a white china teacup with a silver rim which his old landlady had given him as a going-away present, and which he treasured. He hurled it against the corner of the room, where it burst like an electric bulb.

"You bitch!" he screamed, grabbing her by the throat. He choked her. She lay on the floor in his small apartment—

The success of that small story gave me ambitions. I would out-Doyle Conan Doyle. Accordingly, I wrote a story in this vein entitled "Holmes at the Zoo." It went like this:—

There had been a murder. Holmes came in with a torch and three friends. They were going to investigate.

They went into the foundations of the building and found part of it collapsed. They said: He could be in here, hiding. The caretaker pointed out that they themselves had been responsible for the collapse when Holmes had hit a cross-beam with his torch while poking about.

Silence descended like a smell. It opened all the subterranean world, making it bleak as the moon. In the distance a figure could just be made out. He was carrying a large femur bone. When he came within speaking distance he announced that he'd like to present the thigh-bone to the zoo. Holmes, ever alert, said, "Come with me, my man." To test him, he took the femur-bearer to the zoo.

When he got there he told the keeper, "This man wants to give this bone to one of your beasts." The man interrupted: "To the orang-utang," he specified. The keeper thought for a moment. Then he said: "You can't give it to the orang-utang. He's having huge hairy erections and bursts of great energy because of the Vitamin C experiments. We'd like to see how far we can go."

"Aha!" said Holmes, ever sure of himself, almost certain now that he is on the right track.

There. (As you may have noted, I was also attempting to out-Poe Poe.) In any case, with these stories I'd discovered my *métier*. Soon, I moved from the detective story to the story-of-ideas. Then I went on to straight fiction. I'll give you a taste of the former before going on to the latter. This is called "On Speculation":

A middle-aged man spent all his time speculating. It cost him his wife, most of his friends, and would have cost him his children if he'd had any. He speculated on this, he speculated on that. As he walked, he speculated about all he saw, right down to the cracks in the sidewalk. He ended up speculating about speculating. If the mind can question itself, he thought, then what's to stop the mind speculating back? He sat and speculated about the mind speculating about the mind, and tried to figure out where the speculator squeezed in to do his speculating. He found it strange but not incomprehensible. "Now," he thought, as he knocked over an empty garbage can, "if the mind can speculate about the speculator, the speculator the mind, the mind the mind, the speculator the speculator, the thing examined becomes the examiner. So, when I look at my eye it is in fact my eye looking back at me as well." He smiled. "I shall call this 'The Principle of Mutuality.' It is beyond speculation. It is *fact*." He smiled again, until he realized that he had strayed from speculation. He searched for a way out, to turn this *fact* into speculation. But to no avail. He tried speculating about death, his old standby, but he could not concentrate. He tried God. The same. He tried that old walnut, speculating on speculation. Always he could not get beyond that *fact*. His face took on a look of settled desperation. Then it lit up. "I shall speculate about *fact!*" he announced to a black cat that immediately ran under a parked car. He quickened his pace. Right. First, what is beyond *fact?* he speculated, stepping out into the path of an oncoming bus.

So, as I promised I shall now go to the straight fiction. But first, a transition piece, incorporating the detective story *and* the story of ideas. *Then* we hit the main line. Here goes, (and actually, this is a true story, which is a further lead into the main fiction, because everything I write about in my serious fiction is true, absolutely *true*): –

I paid a man $5000 to kill me.

I'd had it. There was nothing I wanted and everything I'd had I might as well not have had.

So I found this guy in a bar, proposed that he put a bullet through my head, told him how, as he had no motive, he wouldn't be caught. He wouldn't even be a suspect, especially since the bar was about empty. He thought I was joking or drunk. But then he thought about it. He'd done nothing like it before, but it seemed like easy money. So he agreed.

Well, just above (in the first sentence, in fact), I said I paid this guy the money. I was going a little fast. I paid him a couple of hundred, downpayment. The rest to be collected after the job was done—I won't bore you with the details. Anyhow, just before I was due to drive out to Bigtop Mountain on the agreed day at the agreed hour, I had a change of heart. I don't know why. Maybe it was just a whim—maybe the decision to do myself in (have myself done in) was a whim in the first place. So I phoned this gentleman and told him the deal was off. He could keep the couple of hundred, just to show I had been serious and was a man of my word.

Well, he didn't like it. He didn't like it one bit. He'd already told his girlfriend they were going to Miami or Vegas or someplace for a month (without, of course, telling her where the money was coming from). He cursed some, calling me an inconsiderate vacillating bastard, a greedy Jew (I'm not even Jewish), and so on, until I hung up. I had to admit he had a point though. It wasn't very considerate. A promise is a promise.

Next day he came round to try and make me reconsider my decision. When I pointed out that, as I had no reason for my first decision, I could have none for this latest inability to consider his pleasure and convenience, he started to rage and finally threatened me.

"I'll kill you just the same, you bastard!" he yelled. "Making me look like a fool!"

"Look," I replied calmly, "the whole thing is not a little ridiculous—"

But he wouldn't let me finish the sentence, and began to throw things—glasses, pillows, tables, Gibbons' *Decline and Fall*, Spengler. After a while, when I saw that reasonable discourse was impossible, I saw a gap with a chink of daylight, and ran towards it.

"Look," I said, "this whole thing is a trick. I still want you to kill me, but by offering the money and then withdrawing it, I figured I could make you feel so angry you'd kill me anyhow. You played right into my hands. Go ahead. Shoot!"

He made a movement with his right forefinger, then realized he didn't have his gun. He was hopping mad, and didn't know if I was telling the truth or not. Either way, he saw me as a pretty cool customer, and since it must have appeared that I really didn't care about my life, as I casually bent over, picking up bits of glass and china, and Gibbons and Spengler; didn't seem to care if I was shot, or strangled, well, right there and then he was lost. Damned if he did and damned if he didn't. So he didn't. Maybe he figured somebody could have seen him come up the drive. In any case, he turned and slammed the door, breaking a small glass window of opaque blue, and knocking Gibbons off his perch again. That was the last I saw of him.

Now I have to figure out what to do with the rest of my life. I've quit playing games. I don't care to live, but then I don't really care to go. I've never done it before, and as I get older I regard it as a bit chancy, not to say downright dangerous. Fortunately, there's nothing much I care to do right now. I look back on my escapade with nostalgia. I knew exactly what was what as I looked at his face contorting and hands twisting.

So now what do I do?

~

And there we'll have to leave him with his predicament. And now for what I promised you before! I am now working on something far more ambitious: a true novel. It begins quietly, lyrically even. It begins like this . . .

"My life is without adventure. I am a creature of habit. Habit has a concentrating effect (as Dr. Johnson said of death). There is too much of everything everywhere. One has to focus on habitual things. There are enough forces for dispersal and distraction."

ABOUT THE AUTHOR

Brian Swann came to the U.S. from England in 1964, becoming a citizen in 1980. He is the author of many books and essays, and is Professor of English at The Cooper Union in New York City.

The Louisville *Courier-Journal* found his 1982 book of fiction, *Unreal Estate* "provocative and haunting." The *North American Review* called his 1981 novella *Elizabeth* "an affecting and strange portrait," while *Library Journal* pronounced it "highly recommended." Of his 1979 collection, *The Runner, The American Book Review* wrote: "This writing deals with something completely different, something intentionally unfocused and previously unacknowledged, something spanking new . . . This is Brian Swann at his finest: a futurist in pursuit of the self's ancient news."

THE PEACEABLE KINGDOM

POEMS

BY

PETER WILD

"Peter Wild makes you come with him. The journey is exciting, a panorama of change and modulation. The quotidian is shadowed by the unusual; the daily is haunted by the mythic and magical. There is no escaping the grip. Movement, energy, an abundance almost squandered. The clauses pile up; we climb with them. And under the virtuosity, the bravura, the comedy, a kind of sadness; a grasp of the way our lives are led. Peter Wild is one of our best poets. This is a rich book."

Brian Swann

OTHER BOOKS FROM ADLER

UPRISING IN EAST GERMANY **and Other Stories**, by Jochen Ziem. First English book-length translation of "one of the few writers of international stature that Germany has produced since Hacks, Grass, and Johnson" *(Times Literary Supplement)*.
$8.95 ISBN 0-913623-07-5

WITTGENSTEIN'S TRACTATUS AND THE MODERN ARTS, by Jorn K. Bramann. A groundbreaking study of the structural similarities between the early classic of Analytic Philosophy and the art, literature, poetry, cinema and architecture of the twentieth century.
$15.95 ISBN 0-913623-05-9

SELF-DETERMINATION: **An Anthology of Philosophy and Poetry**. An "imaginative juxtaposition of philosophers and poets (try to remember the last time you heard Descartes and Goethe, or Hegel and Byron mentioned in the same breath) . . . unearthing long and unjustly overlooked material from Fichte to William Morris to Silesius" (John J. Furlong, Jr.).
$10.95 ISBN 0-913623-00-8

available from

ADLER PUBLISHING COMPANY
P.O. BOX 9342
ROCHESTER, NEW YORK 14604
(716) 377-5804